ONE TO WATCH

HAPPIER EVER AFTER BOOK 1

MACY BUTLER

PARADISE PRESS

For my two teenage sons who took my new calling in stride.

One to Watch

Macy Butler

Printed in the United States of America
First Printing 2019
First Edition 2019

978-0-9852384-1-4

CHAPTER 1

Sally had to shelve books just before closing time because the student worker who was supposed to do the job called in sick. Third time this month, which was annoying, but Sally actually liked the excuse to get out of her office. Too many hours were spent behind that desk these days. Being out among the books reminded Sally of what attracted her to the library in the first place. It certainly wasn't operating budgets, scheduling, and purchasing, which was how she spent most of the hours in the majority of her days. Somehow she had become a prisoner to campus bureaucracy, the desk chair and computer screen her cell. She still liked her job, but it was hard to love it with the passion gone.

It was Sally's lifelong love of books that drove her to pursue the Master's in Library Sciences. Her earliest and fondest childhood memories were of the library. From the age of three, her grandmother took her to the local library for a storytelling hour every Saturday. Sally remembered sitting at her Nana's feet on the colorful rug in the children's book section, captivated by the animated voices and facial expressions of the readers as they brought the stories to life. Once deep into the story, Sally would lean back into her grandmother's shins and close her eyes to listen. The story unfolded against the pinkish black backdrop of her eyelids, the characters vivid in her mind's eye. It was there, in the Lake County Library, that Sally developed her imagination and her wonder of the world. It was a magical time, a magical place.

Sally's mind wandered while the elevator climbed to the medical reference section on the top floor of the library, nostalgic for those mystical childhood times. Sally suspected that those outings initially began as a favor to her mom since they started just after baby Kate came along. Nana kept up the tradition for several years though, and Kate joined once she was old enough to sit semi-still for long enough to hear a story. By then, Sally was able to read some on her own, and Nana would always take a few minutes to let Sally read a story to her and Kate after the official storyteller had finished. Then they would choose a few books for Sally to take home. The seed was planted, and from it, Sally grew into a voracious reader.

The elevator shook gently on its ascent. Sally's fingers traced the ridges on the embossed leather cover of Gray's Anatomy, which was at the top of the stack of just two books on her cart. In her nostalgia, she felt somehow connected to it. She lifted the book to her chest to feel its weight, wanting to feel it closer. She lowered her chin and inhaled the earthy aroma of leather and paper. Memories stirred of her adolescence, whole afternoons spent poring over a stack of books, trying to narrow it down to only two or three she could take home that week. The scent of books was as familiar, and as comforting, as the smell of Nana's kitchen.

The elevator stopped and the doors clambered open. Sally pushed the book cart halfway to the end of the long room and found the spot for the book that had been underneath Gray's Anatomy. After shelving the book, Sally returned to the cart, grabbed the leather-bound anatomy book, and left the clunky cart behind while she headed toward the end of the room.

The stillness of the room swallowed the soft steps of Sally's ballet flats on the carpeted floor as she turned down the second to last aisle to find the book's spot. A faint rustling on the other side of the shelves stopped her before she had reached her destination. It sounded like the wind at first, but no, it was breathing, inhaling, maybe even gasping. Then a whisper, and a faint giggle. Sally held her own breath, waiting. Maybe it was someone on a phone? Then, nothing. After a few seconds of silence, more breathy sounds were followed by a low moan. Sally jerked upright and her face flushed. She knew what was going on over there, and it certainly wasn't reading. It might have had something to do with anatomy, though. Sally nearly laughed out loud at that last thought. She pressed her lips together to keep quiet and cocked her head to the side to listen as the breathy moans continued.

While public displays of affection among horny twenty-year-olds were commonplace around campus, Sally didn't encounter it that often in the library, especially from the confines of her office. Her mind raced: what should she do? Clear her throat and rustle some books on the shelf, to announce her presence and break up the act? That would be the sensible, mature response. Maybe she didn't want to be sensible or mature.

The corners of her mouth tugged upward into an

involuntary smile while she stood as still as a statue with her ear turned upward, listening for more signs of the pleasures happening one aisle over. It was exciting, not only in a naughty *I-shouldn't-be-here* way, but also in a turned-on sexual way. An electric warmth stirred between her legs when the moans started up again. The heat rose upward to her face and her head spun. Intense arousal accented by a tinge of shame. Maybe she was a freak for wanting to eavesdrop on a couple making out, but the tingling in her groin intensified.

It might have been the tingling that made her think of Shane. What would he think of her now, in this perverse position, spying on a couple of coeds and turned on by it? Guilt washed over her like a wave, but as the moans continued, so did the current buzzing through her crotch, and the guilt subsided with the rising tide of arousal. Knowing she shouldn't be there made her want to be there all the more. She tried to imagine who they were, and exactly what they were doing, on the other side of the shelf. She had to see for herself. She just had to. Despite trepidation, legs so numb they felt like someone else's propelled her to the end of the aisle to steal a glimpse.

Sally scooted around to press her back against the shelf's end and stood silent, listening. Beckoning the courage to look around the corner as the muffled moans grew louder, she held her breath and squeezed her eyes shut as she edged ever so slowly to the corner of the next aisle. Afraid to open her eyes for fear they would meet someone else's when she did, Sally pried one eye open just a slit, with sheer will, as she peeked around the corner to find the source of the sounds. A bare white ass, a male ass framed by dark tan lines, moved rhythmically in a telling motion. It was a couple, and they were doing a lot more than making out. Sally covered her mouth to stifle the shriek that nearly escaped, and jerked back into position against the end of the shelf, squeezing her eyes tight. She couldn't unsee that. She didn't want to.

Her heart pounded in her chest and up into her ears. Sally waited for a second more, to be sure they hadn't heard her, then peered around again to drink in the sight of the beautiful couple getting it on among the medical books. Even if only seen from behind, the man was a sight to behold. Tall and lean, with a mop of disheveled blonde curls, his open jeans hung just below his hips, exposing a round, muscular ass that hardened with every thrust into the busty redhead he had pinned against the bookshelf. The woman's white button-down shirt was open to the waist, and her long garnet-colored hair cascaded down the side of her exposed breast, the dark pink of her hardened nipple contrasting against her milky white skin. Wetness spread between Sally's legs.

Despite her height, the woman seemed petite when swallowed up by the broad-shoulders and muscular arms wrapped around her. One hand was behind her head gripping her fiery red mane, while the other cupped her ass, holding her leg up around his waist. With that grip, he pulled her hips closer with every thrust, in and out. The woman's black knit skirt was hiked up around her waist, revealing the full length of her smooth ivory leg leading up to a firm butt cheek. With his back to Sally, and the woman's head thrown back and eyes closed, it felt safe to watch for another minute.

When was the last time she and Shane had sex standing up? Butterflies fluttered in Sally's stomach at the memory of the days they lived in the tiny studio with the single stall shower. The convenient built-in stool in the corner of the shower was the perfect height for supporting a foot in the optimal position for close-quarters upright intercourse. Spontaneous shower sex was far more common for them back then, as was kitchen sex, laundry room sex, and sex in general, come to think of it.

The woman's stifled moans grew louder the harder he pounded her. He hungrily kissed his way up from her neck to her mouth, swallowing her groans as he moved his hand from behind her head to her breast and twirled her nipple between his fingers. Sally's own nipples tingled while moisture trickled steadily into her panties when the man moved his mouth to the woman's hardened nipple while pulling her onto him with every thrust with his grip around her hips. The woman's hair trailed down her back in waves when her head fell back as her moans grew louder, apparently oblivious to her surroundings as her pleasure increased. After a few more pumps, he released the hold around her hips and pulled out of her. Her leg slid down the back of his to find the floor as he moved up to cover her mouth with his.

Sally pulled back instinctively when they changed positions, for fear of being discovered. She stood panting at the end of the aisle, back plastered to the bookshelf, flush with arousal and fear. Christ, what was she doing there? She had lost her ever-loving mind. Would Shane think she was crazy or would he be equally intrigued? Her face burned red and her crotch tingled with the thought of her husband. Her desire to get home to ravage him was stronger in that very moment than she could ever remember. After hearing several seconds of steady, muffled moans coming down the aisle, Sally got the courage to peek around the corner again. She just couldn't resist.

The red-headed beauty pushed her man against the shelf then dropped to kneel before a standing cock that glistened wet with her juices. Even from a distance, it became apparent that the woman's striking red mane was not the only thing in Sally's field of vision that was long and thick. It was undoubtedly one of the nicest cocks Sally had ever seen. Granted, she'd only ever seen five before that one, but still. She longed for a closer view.

Sally's eyes widened when the man's long fingers penetrated the woman's thick hair near the scalp then tightened into fists. The woman's neck arched and she inhaled sharply, but then her lips parted in a wide smile as she stared up to him. She seemed to relish the mix of pleasure and pain. She licked her full lips then ran her tongue around the head of his bulging cock. He bit his lip and groaned as she took the length of his hardness deep into her throat. Perhaps he enjoyed the deep throat action a bit too much, because, after just a few seconds, he pulled her up to him, and whispered something Sally couldn't make out. She suspected it was along the lines of "Wait, Honey, I don't want to come too soon," and nearly giggled out loud.

Sally caught herself, and stood with a hand over her mouth, holding her breath for a few seconds. Of course, she would be mortified if discovered, but the risk made it even hotter. The truth was that more than the fear of being caught watching them, Sally didn't want to interrupt because she wanted the show to go on. The woman leaned in to kiss this man's neck, following the diagonal line from his collarbone up to the sharp angle of his jaw. The chiseled features of his profile were perfectly framed by his messy blonde hair. Underwear model meets stereotypical surfer dude.

He turned the woman by her shoulders and pressed her

softly into the shelf behind her, then dropped to his knees. It was his turn to go down. He pushed her skirt up and she held it high around her waist, exposing a narrow rectangle of trimmed red pubic hair just above the slit of bare lips. Arousal stirred deep within Sally's pelvis when the woman spread her knees open to make space for his head between her legs.

Aside from locker room glimpses in high school, it was the first female genitalia that Sally had seen in real life. She liked the looks of it far more than she would have ever expected. Her face was aflame with the heat of embarrassment mixed with desire. Sally watched his head move slowly at first, then faster as he licked, sucked and nibbled the space beneath the faint red rectangle of pubic hair. The warmth between Sally's legs spread with the woman's gasps and groans. Sally craved Shane's tongue on her clit.

After a couple of minutes, the woman's moans morphed into a low-pitched wail and her hips bucked like a frightened mare. She didn't seem to mind that anyone else on the floor would surely hear her screams. The guy grabbed hold of the tops of her thighs from underneath to keep his mouth attached to her crotch while she flailed in orgasm. Sally's eyes were wide with awe, not only at the incredibly sexy sight but also at the decibel level of the accompanying sounds.

When the wailing diminished to panting, he released her thighs and stood, wiping his mouth on his arm before kissing her. She hugged his neck with both arms as he lifted from under her ass so she could wrap both legs around him. The man turned a quarter turn so Sally had a side view of the action, then lifted the woman up high and thrust his hips forward to position his waiting dick under her glistening pussy. She slid onto him, then he lifted her up nearly off him before lowering her down again, up and down in a heated rhythm. The woman muffled her squeals into his shoulder each time he drove his cock deeper into her.

Sally felt herself clenching the muscles deep in her vagina, which intensified the tingling between her legs. She looked down the long, empty main aisle of the library and contemplated touching herself for a second. She could come at the drop of a hat, and she wanted to, but it was far too risky.

Sweaty and breathless, the man continued the furious rhythm while the gorgeous redhead steadied them with a hand on the shelf until he exploded into her with a final thrust. His low moan sounded like a cat in heat in the distance, muffled as he buried his mouth in her long, ivory neck. Finally, he lifted his chin and rested it on her shoulder, his breath as hard and as fast as his thrusts. The woman blinked her eyes open and started to look around. Sally snapped back to reality and yanked herself back into her hiding position, flattened against the end of the shelf.

Petrified, still clutching the anatomy book that she had never shelved, Sally took a deep breath, trying not to panic. Her mind raced. Her best chance at escaping unnoticed was right then. With a deep breath, she tucked her chin and took off as quickly and as quietly as she could, running on tiptoes toward the elevator. She scurried past the book cart that was halfway there and had to double back to retrieve it. The heavy cart slowed her down, but she pushed herself to keep up speed to try to escape unnoticed before the couple appeared. Her heart pounded in her chest and she could hardly draw a deep breath. She didn’t dare look back.

Sally didn't realize she had been holding her breath until she finally exhaled in relief once she made it to the elevator and pushed the call button. The electricity between her legs charged her entire body. Was she really *that* turned on sexually, or was it the thrill of sneaking around and seeing something she wasn't supposed to? Probably both.

Sally placed the leather bound book back on the cart and took a deep breath to calm her nerves. Happy, giggling voices wafted down the center aisle from the end of the long room. Two seconds later, the voices stopped abruptly for a moment, then continued in a hushed tone. They had seen her. Sally stared straight ahead into the line where the two doors of the elevator met, and bit her lip to stifle a smile. They surely wondered how long she had been there and what she may have heard. Little did they know that she had seen the full show. Heat rose to Sally's face again, and she felt herself clenching the muscles between her legs while she tried not to smile.

The couple was halfway to the elevator when it arrived, so Sally pushed the cart in and held the door for them. It would have been rude not to. The woman entered the elevator first while her boyfriend held the door. Her face was nearly as red as her hair as she strained a smile and a faint hello. Sally noticed that her crystal blue eyes were wide with embarrassment when they met hers as she returned the simple greeting.

The underwear model surfer dude wore a contagious blissful grin. Sally couldn't help but smile. She looked to the floor to hide her flushing face as her cheeks burned hotter, but her gaze wandered back up to the couple while the elevator descended. The woman's beauty was even more striking up close, her porcelain skin and flowing hair nearly too perfect to be real. Her man was equally stunning. His smile widened when his eyes met Sally's for a millisecond, long enough for her to note their emerald color before she averted her gaze.

The sweet, musty smell of sex permeated the small space and stirred the sensations swirling upward from between Sally's legs. She was horny as hell. Thankfully, elevator etiquette allows for silence, so there was no awkward attempt at conversation to add to the strangeness of the situation.

Sally pushed the cart behind the counter and went to grab her coat and keys from the office. She noticed the book still on the cart on her way out. She hadn't finished the task of shelving books, but she did have quite the lesson in anatomy. Sally chuckled as she lifted the book to her nose again. It smelled like home.

CHAPTER 2

Only the sound of Sally's own breath broke the silence on the drive home. The excitement of arousal buzzed through her body, quelled only by the weight of the embarrassment of her perverseness. The longing for touch, for Shane's tongue and cock, was intense, but more than the horniness, Sally yearned to feel the hunger and passion the couple in the library had shared. Sally knew that feeling; she had it once upon a time with Shane. She recalled it like a distant memory, though, the way she remembered the red bicycle with streamers flowing from the ends of banana handle bars that she received on her fifth birthday. Almost as though it had happened to someone else, it was so long ago. She was the same coy lover who could seduce her husband in ten seconds flat, but those seductive skills had been shelved like the heavy books in the medical reference section.

A sliver of light sliced through the dark bedroom to illuminate the rhythmic rise and fall of Shane's chest. Sally was wired with excitement and wanted to tell him what she had seen. Why couldn't he be awake, dammit? Maybe it was better that he was asleep. She might not be able to get past the embarrassment of admitting that she had watched the entire sex act. It was really quite naughty of her. She kind of liked feeling naughty, though. Would Shane like it too? Would he enjoy seeing his sensible, predictable, responsible Sally, as a something of a pervert?

Sally tiptoed across the room, around the dresser, and into the bathroom to get ready for bed. She tied her dark blonde hair up into a messy bun while the shower heated. Even with eyes closed, Sally couldn't shake the image of the hot couple. She pulled her navy blue below-the-knee dress over her head and tossed it into the basket in the corner. She watched herself push her yellow cotton briefs to the floor in the mirror and giggled at the sight of her own pussy. It was a barely-tamed bush by comparison to the redhead's smooth, sleek lips. Sally rubbed her palm over the furry light-brown triangle. It was probably outdated, but pubic hairstyle trends had never been on her radar. Was it a generational thing or was she just too prudish and practical to get a Brazilian wax job like she had seen tonight?

Those kids weren't *that* much younger than Sally, yet she always thought of them as kids. It wasn't just an age thing. Surely some thirty-two-year-olds also shaved their pussies. Hell, some may even be crazy or adventurous enough to fuck in libraries. Sally just wasn't one of them, and never had been.

Sally studied her naked body in the mirror. Not bad. She ran the backs of her fingers alongside her perky boobs and down her slender waist to the sides of her round ass. When steam filled the air, Sally stepped under the hot stream. Her favorite thing about a shower before bed was lathering up in the lemongrass-scented shower gel Shane gave her every year for her birthday. When Sally's hands slid over her breasts, a surprising zing from her nipple down to her crotch caught her off guard. Sally rubbed her nipples again to check the reaction. The electric impulse shot through her again, directly to the sweet spot between her legs.

Instinctively, Sally moved a hand there and started to massage the soft mound. She parted her lips, slid her slick fingers into the slit and found her hardened clit begging for attention. She flicked her wet finger over the stiff nub, but the direct stimulation was too much to bear, so Sally moved her finger around the base of her clit instead. It had been ages, maybe even a year, since she last touched herself like that. Circling around the edges of her clit caused the tingling to brew intensely. Her pleasure spot was ready to explode. Sally had to pull her hand away to steady herself on the wall. Her legs trembled under her.

Sally leaned back on the tile wall to catch her breath and questioned her trepidation. She was on the verge, and wanted to come, so why did she stop? It was almost as if the prospect of the orgasm scared her, a pleasure so intense it bordered on pain. Her eyes followed the stream of hot water up to the showerhead, which gave her an idea. Sally removed the handheld shower attachment and changed the dial to pulse, then directed the stream between her legs. She leaned back on to the tile wall and fondled her breast with her free hand, moaning while the jet pounded rhythmically on her swollen clit. Half a minute later, Sally was squirming under the stream. Within a few seconds more, she erupted in orgasm. She suppressed the urge to scream out in ecstasy and instead bit her lip and groaned as quietly as possible. She had never come so quickly in her life. She usually had to work for it. Or, more accurately, Shane did.

Sally was still tingling all over when she slipped into bed beside her sleeping husband. She snuggled up behind him to spoon him, and resisted the urge to stroke his cock to try to wake him up. Shane had an early lecture the next morning, but maybe he wouldn't mind the sleep disruption if it was for sex. He'd be shocked, that's for sure. She hadn't woken him for sex since before they were married, and never sober. It was tempting, but she couldn't do it.

CHAPTER 3

Sally snuck up behind Shane when she found him in the kitchen pouring coffee and snaked her arms around to grip his solid pectorals. He stiffened in surprise at first, then softened and turned, his eyes narrow with curiosity.

She planted a deep kiss on his lips then stepped back to take in the sight of him. He looked sexy in his jacket and tie, so professional. It was still a thrill to see him dressed like a professor after eight years of jeans and T-shirts while studying for his Ph.D. Something about a man in a tie turned Sally on.

"Well, good morning." There was a tinge of doubt in his voice as she rubbed her butt through the soft satin of her robe. "Lucky you, still in your bathrobe. I suppose you deserve it after working a double shift yesterday. How'd it go?"

"Oh, great. It went great." Sally's heart fluttered. Great didn't quite capture how well her night had gone.

"Great? Well, that's good to hear. You usually take two days to recover from those late shifts. But you look wide awake and ready to go."

It was true, she had been ready to go since witnessing that sexy scene in the library. "Yeah, I guess I slept well. I feel good."

Shane kissed her on the lips then brushed her hair away from her face and tucked it behind her ear. "You look good, too. You have plans for your day off today?"

Sally beamed with a silly grin. She ran her hand up the inseam of his crotch and gently stroked his cock while leaning in to whisper in his ear. "We could enjoy it together before you go to work."

Shane eyed her suspiciously, then looked over her shoulder to scan the room.

Sally played along and smiled while she looked around, too. "What? What are you looking for?"

Shane grinned. "I'm looking for my wife. It seems someone replaced her with a horny devil."

Sally stepped even closer and pulled Shane closer by the lapel of his tweed jacket. "I hope you like the replacement." Sally was straddling one of Shane's legs so she could rub herself up and down his thigh.

Shane's cock enlarged inside his khaki slacks and pressed into Sally. "Oh yeah? Is she here to stay?"

"Maybe so." Sally smiled and continued to stroke Shane through his pants.

Shane inhaled deeply and slid his hands down the silky robe to give Sally's ass a squeeze. Sally pressed her crotch harder onto his thigh. "Really, babe, why now? I mean, I have class in 20 minutes. Now I've got a half chubby. You're torturing me."

"Maybe you could be just a little late for class?" She squeezed his nearly hard cock. She wanted to suck it. A flash of the redhead going down on the hot surfer dude the night before made Sally gasp as she nibbled Shane's ear.

Shane looked up toward the ceiling and shook his head. He leveled his eyes on hers then reluctantly pushed her hips away, peeling her off his thigh. "As much as I would love to, and I would really, really love to, I can't. This is my Physics 421 class. You know I'm the only first-year professor to get to teach a senior level class. And these guys take it so seriously. I have to go."

"That's what I get for marrying a rocket scientist." Sally grabbed his dick again. "I'll be here when you get back."

"Oh wow, well, I, I hope so." His voice went up an octave as he spoke, like a pubescent teen, so he cleared his throat. "I guess this is what I get for marrying a librarian?" The sarcasm in his voice was palpable.

"I guess so. You never know with those librarians." Really, he had no idea.

Shane raised his eyebrows and studied her face suspiciously again. "Right. You never know. But, hey, If aliens did replace my wife with you, can you ask them to leave you here at least until after I come home from work?"

Sally put on her best robotic voice. "I'll be sure to pass on the message to my leader." She kissed Shane on the cheek and patted his ass as he started for the door.

Sally giggled as she watched Shane pause outside the front door and shift while tugging at the crotch of his khakis to rearrange his package. He was obviously both shaken and aroused by her unusual friskiness that morning.

It wasn't that there was anything *wrong* with their sex life. They had sex once a week, usually, maybe a week and a half if they were busy or tired. Sometimes they did it twice a week, normally only if there was a special occasion, which usually involved alcohol. Sex was great when they had it, and neither of them really had reason to complain. Sally knew how to do exactly what Shane needed, and he knew how to push her buttons, too. It was highly unusual, though, for Sally to be so horny, especially first thing in the morning. It just wasn't her nature.

Sally poured herself a cup of coffee and stared out the window over the kitchen sink. The sky was brighter and the grass greener than it had been the day before, she was sure of it. Sally had planned to be productive that day, cleaning out her closet and organizing the attic to separate items to donate to a community yard sale that was coming up in a couple of weeks. Screw that. It was far too nice a day to waste. She daydreamed of indulging in a morning of leisure instead. Her feet were a sad sight, and sandal season was right around the corner. She would go for coffee and a pedicure. She deserved it.

CHAPTER 4

The buzz of the massaging pedicure chair awakened the tingling current that had been vibrating through her since the night before. A smile spread across her lips as Sally noticed the specials listed on the chalkboard at the reception area of the salon. One, in particular caught her eye. *All waxing 25% off.*

Sally had never had a bikini wax, let alone a Brazilian. The only waxing she had ever done was a lower leg wax, several years earlier, which she found ridiculously painful and not at all rewarding. Shaving was much easier and more practical, so that's what she did.

The vivid memory of the trimmed red rectangle over smooth lips returned. Her heart rate quickened. Maybe waxing wasn't as bad as she made it out to be. Maybe she should give it another chance. She pushed herself forward in the pedicure chair, smiled and waved a hand to call the spa manager over.

"Yes, dear, what can I do for you?"

Sally's throat constricted, so she struggled to get the words out. "I wonder, does your special on waxing apply to a Brazilian?" Her voice had subconsciously dropped to nearly a whisper by the last word. She looked around to see if anyone had heard.

"Sure it does. Would you like to book one?"

Why not? Why the hell not. Her heart raced. Sally swallowed hard. "Can you do it now? After my pedicure, I mean?"

"Yeah, I think so. Let me check." A couple of minutes later, she returned with the good news that they could accommodate Sally's Brazilian.

Sally waited in a small room, sitting upright on the treatment table wearing only her shirt and a small towel covering her private parts. A smiling middle-aged Asian woman let herself in and said hello while she gently folded the towel into a strip.

"Oh, it's first time? First Brazilian?"

Sally chuckled. Her bush had given it away. "Yes, first time. Does it hurt?"

"First time hurt a little, not much. Don't worry. I make it fast. You know how you want? You want leave some hair, or no hair?"

Sally struggled momentarily to find meaning in the words. "Oh, yes, some hair, please."

"Okay, how you want?" The woman handed Sally a laminated card from the drawer of the table behind her. There were six drawings of different pubic hair styles. Triangles, diamonds, hearts, squares. Sally pointed to the thin rectangle, labeled Landing Strip.

"Okay. Now lay down." She pushed Sally's shoulder gently back toward the table.

"Good. Now bend legs." She tapped under Sally's knees until they bent, then kept tapping near her feet. "Now make legs like frog, feet together, knees open." Sally bent her knees but held them together. The woman wedged a hand between Sally's knees, and when they parted, she pulled the towel off, exposing Sally's unruly pubes. Nothing like getting right down to business. Heat flooded her face as she stared at the ceiling.

The woman spread warm wax on one side of Sally's bikini line with a popsicle stick then applied a firm pressure that was almost relaxing, for a nanosecond. But she quickly followed with, "Now I pull," and she did. Sally gasped at the sudden shooting pain. Holy shit, that hurt.

The woman moved around the opposite side of the table and patted Sally on the arm. "Sorry, sorry. First time hurts. This side not so bad."

Sally held her breath and squeezed her hands into fists while the woman spread the wax. It was true, the other side wasn't so bad, as it was less a surprise. When she reapplied the wax further back toward her ass, it was pretty terrible, though. But it was true, she made it quick. Sally released the breath she had been unintentionally holding when the woman tapped the side of her thigh. She had survived. Or so she thought.

"Okay, now on side."

"Excuse me?"

"Roll over, on side."

Wait, there was more? Jesus. "Ah, okay." Sally did as she was told.

"Now spread cheek." The woman pressed upward on the top butt cheek to open the gap between them, and guided Sally's hand there with her other one. "You hold. I wax." Sally held the cheek up as instructed. The woman spread the wax along both sides of her crack.

Sally hadn't bargained for the back bit. How embarrassing. And painful. She bit her lip and winced audibly when the wax was ripped off. "Ouch!"

"Sorry, sorry" The woman patted Sally's butt cheek gently. "Okay, back on your back, let's see did we get it all." Sweat beaded on her brow as Sally rolled over. She fucking better have gotten it all. Sally couldn't handle any more.

"Okay make frog legs again. Good. Now lift knees so I can see." The woman tapped upward under Sally's ankles. Sally pressed her palms into her hands as she lifted her feet. She wanted to crawl into a hole when the lady lowered her head under Sally's dangling feet to examine her anus.

"Sorry, sweetie. We miss some hairs." She laughed as she tapped the side of her ass. "Your big cheeks hide some."

What the hell? "No, no, it's okay, just leave it." No fucking way was she bearing any more of this pain or embarrassment. Sally was already moving to the edge of the table to sit up. "I'm sure it's fine."

"No, we can't leave like that. Don't worry, almost finish. Turn over, on your knees now. Hands and knees."

Sally stared at her with wide eyes, motionless, but soon realized that the woman wasn't taking no for an answer. She wasn't finished, even if Sally was. Sally reluctantly climbed back on the table to hands and knees facing the woman, who chuckled again while she made a small circle in the air with her index finger. The knot tightened in Sally's stomach with the next command. "Now turn around."

Sally stood on her knees and pivoted to turn her back to the lady. She squeezed her eyes shut as she went down to her hands, sticking her ass in the woman's face. No one had ever seen her from this angle, so up close and personal, not even Shane.

Sally could feel the warmth of the bulb as the attendant adjusted the light to illuminate her wide-open lady bits. The woman pulled her cheeks apart again and spread the wax on both sides, then ripped it off in one continuous motion. Humiliation had numbed Sally to the pain by then.

"Now, finish. See, not so bad. Good job. Looks nice." The woman patted her on the bottom and quietly left the room. Sally's legs trembled as she stood. She took a handheld mirror from the counter and opened her knees to examine the new look.

The light brown landing strip was not as pronounced as she expected, maybe because it was overshadowed by the redness and swelling of the inflamed tissue around it. Sally touched the skin, expecting it to hurt, but found it nearly numb. It looked, and felt, like someone else's pussy in the mirror. An alien pussy. She laughed as she dressed. Shane might get his alien experience after all.

Even though the positioning was mortifying, and the pain excruciating, Sally knew she would love the results of the Brazilian once the swelling and redness subsided. Shane would too.

CHAPTER 5

Sally stopped in her tracks. She was not a lingerie kind of girl, but, for some reason, the red and black ensemble in the window of the Hot and Bothered Boutique caught her eye.

Her eyes moved up from the mannequin's blunt plastic toes to the sexy black lace panties trimmed in red, then further upward to the matching underwire bra. Eying the off-white plastic visible through the bra made her think of her nipples showing through the delicate lace. A prickly tingle stirred around her own nipples, and a warmth brewed deep in her groin, moistening her sensible and sporty pink cotton panties. Sally sipped her iced mocha latte and tried to stifle the smile that tugged at the corners of her lips. Getting horny thinking about nipples. That was certainly a first.

The only black lace anything that Sally owned was a bra that her sister had given her as a birthday gift three or four years earlier. She hated that bra; it was so scratchy and uncomfortable. Shane felt differently. He had nearly ripped it off her the first time she wore it. Sally chewed her straw and blushed at the memory as she admired the lace set on the mannequin. Had she deprived Shane of sexy lingerie all these years? He hadn't ever suggested it, nor had he ever bought her any. But he did seem to like it a lot, that time.

It had been a very long time since Shane had last ravaged her like he did those years ago in the black lace bra. It had been years since she had really wanted to be ravaged, truth be told. She liked sex, but she didn't really crave it, or, rather, she hadn't craved it in a long, long time. Something was different now, though. The tingling in her crotch that awakened with the slightest provocation, for one thing. Sex constantly on her mind, for another.

Sally studied the lingerie, convincing herself. Maybe this little black lace number would be more comfortable than that itchy bra so that she'd actually *want* to wear it. Shane would like it, no doubt. A butterfly gently fluttered in her stomach. She would, too. Out of nowhere, Sally envisioned herself wearing the lingerie under an open trench coat in the library, and Shane fucking her against a bookshelf. She nearly dropped her iced latte.

Sally gaze dropped to the ground and she struggled for a deep breath as she shook her head, trying to clear the impure thoughts. Her shiny red toes distracted her. She wiggled them in her sandals. The new color would match the red ribbon trim on the lingerie set perfectly. It was a sign from the universe: she had to try it on. The doorbell chimed as Sally entered the store.

Somehow the impromptu "me time" on her morning off work, intended only to be a pedicure and a coffee, had turned risqué. Starting with her first-ever Brazilian wax, and now, lingerie shopping. There was a lightness to the morning, as though she was floating through it. Sally felt a little naughty. Feeling naughty felt good.

"Let me guess, a small? And a C cup?" Sally's face warmed at the question from the soft voice that appeared beside her at the rack. The petite woman in a high-necked silk shirt peered through the tiny glasses on the end of her nose, trying to make out the minuscule letters on the ticket in her hand. She could be her grandmother.

Sally eyed her own chest, cheeks ablaze with embarrassment. "Um, yes, actually. A 32C, please. How did you know that?"

"After thirty years sizing women up, I guess pretty well." The old woman rifled through the rack and pulled out a size small panties, then continued to search for the right size in the bra. "We just got these in this week. Really nice, aren't they? I think the best thing about these sets is that they are practical enough to double as everyday undergarments, but sexy enough for the bedroom, too." Sally giggled under her breath at the way she raised her eyebrows when she said "bedroom".

Sally took the two hangers the clerk held out for her. She tried to imagine donning the racy combo under her librarian work attire, or beneath the yoga pants and tank tops that she pretty much lived in when not at the library. Yeah right. It was nothing like her usual bras and panties, which were nearly all practical, one-hundred-percent-cotton pieces. But the lace did feel nice. She rubbed the fabric gently on her cheek. "Wow, it's really soft." Not at all scratchy.

"Yes, it's the finest French lace, and the trim is real silk, not satin."

Sounded expensive. Sally checked the ticket. Yes, it was.

She slipped into the dressing room, and out of her jeans and tee shirt. Her pink cotton panties covered every interesting bit, and her plain white cotton bra was puritanical beside the lace one on the hanger. She smiled at herself in the mirror. Average height, average weight, completely average. Cute, but boring. Did she only notice her mediocrity now that she wanted to break away from it?

Sally brushed the hair back from her face and tucked it behind her ear. She watched herself in the mirror, pushing her panties down over her knees to the floor. The playful twinkle she glimpsed in her eyes was as unfamiliar as the sight of her newly-coiffed lady bits. She stared into the eyes in the mirror, her own and yet somehow unfamiliar, while she unhooked her bra and shook it off her shoulders. The cool air made her nipples contract into erect little points on her round breasts. Instinctively Sally raised her hands to cover her boobs. Her palms brushing her nipples sent a sudden jolt straight to her crotch, just like in the shower last night. She was getting wetter by the second.

On second thought, she should probably keep her panties on underneath the ones she was trying on, like she did when shopping for swimsuits. Embarrassed by her nudity and her horniness, Sally stooped to pull her panties up and caught sight of her flushed face in the mirror. The color of her cheeks matched the pink of her panties and her nipples. The electric warmth pulsed between her legs.

Maybe she was she ovulating. That might help explain her extreme horniness. It couldn't all be a result of what she had seen the night before, surely not. There must be more to it than that. Sally often noticed an increased interest in sex when she was mid-cycle.

Sally cynically viewed the increased libido that came with

ovulation as Mother Nature trying to trick her into having a baby, and she was not falling for it. When was her last period anyway? She wrinkled her brow while making a quick mental count. Nope, that was last week. That horny feeling was coming from what she had seen at work the night before. There was no other explanation. She had been tingling all over and giddy ever since.

That horny feeling had no doubt been what motivated the new hairdo down there, and was surely the reason Sally lingered by the window of the lingerie shop. Sally wasn't complaining. She loved the new pubic style, and since she still had her pink cotton briefs underneath, she could only imagine how sexy it would be clad in just the new black lace thong panties. Sally couldn't wait for Shane to see it. He already suspected she'd been replaced by an alien. When he saw her newly coiffured pussy, he would be convinced.

Sally turned to the side to get a different view of her breasts in the black lace bra. Her eyes honed in on her pink nipples visible through the lace. The underwire lifted her boobs enough to create an attractive cleavage. Sally sucked her bottom lip and tilted her head as she traced the cleft down to the delicate silk bow between her breasts, scanning the area from her neck to her waist. Amazing the difference a bra made. She looked like a totally different person.

The black lace and red ribbon ensemble fit Sally to a tee, so she bought her first ever sexy underwear set. She was giddy with excitement when leaving the store, and had to tell someone, so she called Kate.

CHAPTER 6

"Hey, sis, you'd be so proud of me."

"Oh yeah, why's that? Wait, let me guess... you got a tattoo?" Kate's voice was dripping with sarcastic enthusiasm.

"What? No! I'd never get a tattoo. You know that."

"Yeah, I know. It was a joke. There are *so* many things you'd never do. We have to work on that." Kate loved to make fun of her sister's more conservative nature. "Anyway, don't leave me hanging. What's the surprise?"

"I bought some sexy lingerie."

"Wow, that's huge, Sal. I mean, for you." Again with the sarcasm. "So, what's it like? Latex? Leather?"

"No, I said lingerie, not an S & M costume. Jeez, Kate, not everyone's a freak like you."

"Yeah, well you could stand to be a little more freaky like me, Sally. It would do you some good. You only live once."

Sally shook her head. "Yeah, yeah, I know, YOLO. Your motto."

"Damn right. Now, seriously, tell me about your racy lingerie."

Racy was not really the word for it. It seemed suddenly ordinary after Kate's guessing game. "Oh, never mind. You'll just make fun of me."

"Don't be silly. Come on. You can take it, can't you, Sal? After all those years of picking on me when we were kids, surely you can handle a little of it now?"

"Me picking on you? Well if I did, it's because you were an annoying little tattle tale, and totally deserved it."

"That's probably true." Kate laughed. "But you were also a bitchy bully, so it was fun to tell on you. Come on, tell me about your sexy clothes."

"Okay, it's a black lace bra and panties set with the prettiest red ribbon trim. Real silk ribbon trim, and the softest lace."

"Wow, you really went way out of your comfort zone, didn't you? Good job, sis." Try as she may, Kate couldn't not make fun of Sally. So many years of bashing one another.

"Fuck you! I should have known better than to tell you." Sally laughed. "It's really cute! And it's see-through, top and bottom. I thought you'd be proud. The only lingerie I owned before today was that black lace bra that you bought me for my birthday."

"Are you serious? That was what, like five years ago? And just so you know, a bra hardly counts as lingerie, in the sexy sense of the word."

"Well, when all your other bras are cotton, it does."

Kate chuckled. "God, Sally, you really do need to kink it up a little. Poor Shane."

What do you mean, poor Shane? He likes me how I am."

"Oh, I know he loves you dearly. And I know you guys are vanilla as can be, but I'm sure that he'd love for you to kink up for him, at least a little bit."

"Vanilla? What does that even mean?"

"See, you're so vanilla, you don't even know you're vanilla."

Sally really had no idea what Kate was talking about, but she was pretty sure it was meant to be an insult. "As opposed to what? Chocolate?"

Kate laughed. "As opposed to *not* vanilla. You know, kind of kinky. Fringe."

"Oh, you mean freaky?"

"Yeah, maybe. Get freaky, sis."

"That was kind of the idea, I guess. In so far as lingerie can be freaky."

"Well, it's all relative. It's freaky for you, I suppose. Hey, where are you now? Are you still out? I just finished a meeting and have a couple of hours free. Wanna do lunch?"

"Sure, I don't have any plans. Other than the work I was supposed to do at home. Lunch sounds way more fun. How about the Asian bistro near your office?" The morning of leisure was turning into a full day of fun.

Kate's face lit up at the sight of her sister and the shopping bag in her hand as Sally approached the table by the window.

"Ooh, is this it?"

"Yes, ma'am." Sally handed her the bag. "Be discreet, please. You don't have to make a show of it."

"Oh, alright." Kate opened the bag. "Hey, I ordered for us both already. I got the Thai chicken salad that you like. Hope you don't mind, but I'm hungry." Kate's eyes widened as she lifted the panties from the bag. "Oh, these are really nice, very see-through." She raised her eyebrows suggestively. "And the red ribbon trim is really cute. This cut will look great on your butt," she complimented.

Sally blushed. The butt with the big cheeks that had complicated the wax job. "Thanks. I love the bottoms but check the top. It's even cuter."

Kate pulled the bra out, turning her back to the room to block it from view so she could hold it up and study it discreetly. "Wow, this is really sexy. I don't think it will hide your nipples at all under clothes, so it may not work so well as a bra, per se, but it will definitely look great with no other clothes on. Shane is going to love this!"

With her back to the room, Kate was facing the window, holding the bra up with a huge grin on her face. Since she was focused on Sally, Kate didn't notice the hot young guy walking by the restaurant window. He stopped to stare, smiling right back at the pretty girl in the window holding sexy underwear. Sally giggled when she noticed him. Kate followed Sally's gaze and found herself staring the handsome man right in the eyes. Kate's face turned as red as the cute ribbon trim. She shoved the bra back into the bag and turned to face Sally, lifting her hand to shade her face on the side of the window. The cute guy waited a few seconds, then gave up and moved on.

"Oh my god, why didn't you tell me he was there? Is he gone

yet?" Kate seemed to be practicing her ventriloquist skills, moving her lips as little as possible while she whispered.

"I didn't see him until just before you did. And yes, he's gone." Sally had to laugh. "It's funny to see you embarrassed, for once."

Kate lowered her hand and relaxed into her usual nonchalant self. "Yeah, it doesn't happen often. He was hot, though. If he hadn't been hot, I wouldn't have cared." It was true.

The waiter delivered their salads, along with a bottle of white wine.

"Did you order this?" Sally motioned toward the wine in the silver bucket on the stand beside the table.

"Of course I did. I knew you'd say no if I asked, so I didn't."

Sally looked at her watch. Was she really going to start drinking at 12:40 on a Wednesday?

"Oh, come on. Live a little."

"I know, YOLO. Alright, I'll have a glass. Just one." The waiter served them both, but Kate grabbed the bottle after he put it in the bucket and filled Sally's glass to the brim before she could protest.

"If you're only going to have one, you better make it a good one." Kate lifted her glass for a toast. "Here's to getting your kink on, one pair of panties at a time."

Sally carefully clinked Kate's glass so as not to spill her overflowing one, then slurped the wine from the top to lower the level so she could make her own toast. "And to new hairdo's."

Kate lifted her glass again, her eyes narrowing while she

studied Sally's hair. It looked the same as usual, of course, since there was nothing different to detect. Sally grinned back at Kate, her eyes dancing with an unusual playfulness.

Kate cocked her head, obviously confused. "Are you going to get your hair done? Or did you? If you did, I'd say you should go a little more drastic if you want it noticed."

"Yeah, I got a new do at the salon this morning, you just can't see it."

Kate's eyes slanted further, her curiosity apparently piqued by Sally's mysterious manner. "Okay, sis, I'm stumped. What the hell are you talking about?"

Sally sipped her wine again before answering, savoring the rare moment of mystique. Kate had often shocked Sally with tales of wild sexual escapades and other adventures, but since Sally rarely surprised, she wanted to drag it out. "Here's a hint: You can see the new style much better when I'm wearing my new outfit," Sally glanced toward the shopping bag. It took a few seconds, then Kate's face lit up with the realization. She even blushed briefly as she burst into giggles.

"Oh wow, Sal, what did you get done? A bikini wax?"

Sally nodded. "Uh huh, like they do in Brazil."

Kate nearly spit her wine back into her glass. "Whoa, that's a shocker!"

"Not as vanilla as you thought?"

"Plenty of vanilla people get their hoo-ha waxed, Sally. You have to do more than that to freak it up."

"I'd say it's a good start."

Kate giggled with her. "At least you're trying. That alone is astounding. Does Shane know yet?"

"No, it was a spur of the moment decision. There was a special at the salon and I felt like doing something different."

Kate raised her eyebrows in surprise, then looked down, picked up her fork, and started on her salad without a word. Sally scanned Kate's face for a clue to her sudden shutdown, but could see nothing beyond the mask of her neutral expression. Sally pushed her salad around on her plate, not a bit hungry. She felt the blood drain from her face and she shifted nervously in her seat as she pretended to eat while contemplating her sister's silent treatment. Quiet reserve was not Kate's style. Something was definitely going on with her, but what? Maybe she shouldn't have told her. They told each other everything, but it was usually Kate sharing the juicy tidbits. Sally rarely had much to tell. But it was only lingerie and a wax job, for crying out loud. Why would that make her sister act weird.

Finally, Kate looked up from her salad and took a deep breath after a sip of wine. Sally held her breath awaiting her sister's commentary. "So, what brought this on, Sal? I mean, it's really unusual for you. Did something happen to trigger this? Is everything okay with you and Shane?"

Sally's face scrunched up in confusion. Something had triggered this, indeed, but Kate had no idea about that. And what was she thinking it had to do with Shane? "What do you mean?"

Kate leaned across the table and whispered. "Did you meet someone?"

When Sally processed what Kate had suggested, she stared

back at her in disbelief "What? No! Shane and I are fine. I just decided to do something different. That's all."

Kate finished her first glass of wine and poured a second. Without asking, she topped off Sally's glass as well. Sally was too shocked by the implication to protest.

"Sorry, sis, I hope that didn't offend you. I didn't think that you would go there, really, but it's just so unusual, all of it. The lingerie, the Brazilian. It seemed like you were inspired by something, by *someone*."

Sally couldn't be mad, since, technically, it was true. "No, it's okay. I understand. It is pretty weird. For me, especially." Sally sipped her wine nervously.

"Ha! Yeah. Totally unexpected." Kate's brief smile left as quickly as it had appeared; her face turned serious. "But you know you could tell me anything, right? I mean, I won't judge you. You should know that. For all that I've told you, and you always accept me." Kate reached across the table to squeeze Sally's hand.

Sally took a long draw off her glass of wine. She felt the warmth of it in her belly and the tingling buzz feeling that branched out from it. "Thank you for saying that, Kate. Really. I value your friendship and I do know I could count on you if I had a secret like that to tell."

"Well, that's a relief."

"But really, things are great for me and Shane. He's finally doing what he loves, and I'm happy at work, too. The house projects are under control. Everything is going really well for us."

"Well when you say it like that, it sounds like your normal, boring happy life. Which makes me happy. So, do you have a plan on how to unveil this surprise to Shane?"

"Oh, I don't know, something sappy I guess. You know, light some candles, soft music, wait for him in the bedroom, wearing the lingerie, of course."

"He's going to flip his lid when he sees you in that! And when he sees you *out* of that, whoa, watch out!" Kate's excitement showed in the increasing volume of her voice.

Sally laughed but looked around to see who may have heard. Kate was acting more than a little buzzed. Sally was getting there, too. She'd better slow down. It must have been the wine that compelled her to explain further.

"You know, you were right, though. I was inspired by something."

Kate raised her eyebrows and tilted her head. "Oh really?"

"I saw something last night."

Kate's grin took over her face. "Well go on! Do tell."

Sally sipped her wine. Liquid courage. "I had to work a double yesterday, so I was in the library late. The student worker who normally does the grunt work called in sick, so I had to return the reference books at the end of the night. When I was up on the top floor shelving the last of the books, I heard sounds coming from the last aisle. When I looked to see what it was, I saw a couple there."

"A couple? What were they doing?" Kate was playing dumb but Sally suspected she just wanted to make her come out and say it.

"They were making out. Actually, they were having sex." She

sipped her wine slowly and took a deep breath before continuing. "They were really hot."

Kate leaned in across the table, wide eyes begging for detail. "So what did you do?"

"What do you mean what did I do? I just stood there."

"So you didn't interrupt them? And you didn't turn and run away? You mean, you just stood there and *watched*?"

Was that accusation in Kate's voice? Was she judging her? "Um, yeah, I watched." Sally's face was on fire.

"For how long?" Kate's eyes twinkled and her grin widened.

"Long enough. Until they finished."

"Well, was that a long time, or were they nearly finished when you found them?" Kate loved to see Sally squirm. Bitch.

"It was quite a while. I got a good look at pretty much everything." There. She'd said it. Beads of sweat tickled her forehead.

Kate leaned back in her chair and uncrossed then re-crossed her legs as her eyes leveled on Sally's. "You little voyeuristic vixen."

Sally leaned in and whispered, "I know, I couldn't help myself. It was unreal. I couldn't not watch." She pressed her crossed legs together as she continued, squeezing her inner thighs into one another. "They were both so beautiful. She had this gorgeous long red hair. And he was tall and lean, with messy blond curls. He looked like a surfer."

Kate pressed for more details. "What else did you see? Were they dressed?"

"Kind of. She was in a skirt, which was pushed up around her waist, and her top was unbuttoned so her boobs were out. His pants were down enough to free his, um, ample manhood." Sally cleared her throat. Just thinking about it made her horny again.

Kate sipped her wine and giggled, shaking her head. "I can't believe you. That is just too funny. And now, look at you, buying lingerie and getting your snatch waxed!"

"Yeah, I guess I was inspired, like you said."

"Why? Was the redhead's snatch waxed, too?" Kate's eyebrows rose and her eyes widened. "Did you see her pussy?"

Sally had never felt so embarrassed in all her life. Her face burned and she held her breath, not sure how to answer. Truth seemed the only way to go, this far in, but it escaped in barely a whisper. "Yeah. I hadn't ever seen one in real life."

"Dear lord." Kate shook her head and smiled, completely relaxed and nonjudgmental in her demeanor, back to her usual self. "I take it you haven't told Shane about your peep show either, then?"

"No. Actually, I really wanted to, but he was asleep when I got home." Should she tell her sister about the fun she had with herself in the shower? No, definitely TMI. She had shared more than enough already.

"Will you tell him?"

"I don't know. Maybe. But do you think he'll be weirded out by it? Or think I'm a freak for being so inspired after watching."

"Sally, I don't think he will care what inspired you when he sees you in that black lace ensemble with your new smooth pussy."

Sally felt the flutter of embarrassment in her stomach at hearing her sister refer to Sally's genital as a "pussy." She really was a prude, wasn't she? Was, as in past tense. She felt herself shedding that skin, already a little wilder, a little kinkier. And she liked it.

"You're probably right. He might even get a kick out of it, to be honest. He's always been a lot more adventurous than me, in that respect." Shane tried to get her to watch porn back when they were dating. She just couldn't do it. She felt almost disgusted by it, the way the women acted, the way they were treated.

Kate chuckled. "Isn't everyone?"

"Ha, that coming from you isn't even an insult." Sally sipped the last of her wine and eyed the bottle, still a quarter full. Why not? She poured herself half of what was left. The midday buzz and the sexy talk with her sister was fun. "I don't aspire to your level of freakdom."

Kate laughed and raised her glass to Sally. "You don't know the half of it, Sis."

"I don't doubt that, at all. I don't even *want* to know the full extent of your freakiness, I'm sure." They clinked glasses again. "But since we're sharing secrets, tell me one."

Kate giggled, also enjoying the wine buzz. "You already know my secrets. I think yours are enough for today."

"Oh come on, you said yourself that I don't know the half of it. Surely there's a little secret you can share."

Kate studied her sister's face while swirling the wine in her glass. "Well, your story reminded me of the time that I discovered that I like to watch, too." Kate paused for effect while her sister stared, willing her to continue with wide eyes. "I was at a party a couple of years ago, a sort of wild party. By the end of the night, there were people having sex out in the open. I was shocked at first, but then I was really turned on by it."

Sally's jaw dropped and she stared at her sister with a gaping mouth and eyes so wide they looked scared. "What? What people? What party? You mean a couple just randomly started having sex, in front of everyone else, like out in the open?"

"Not exactly. Let's just say it was a very open-minded crowd."

Sally's brow wrinkled as she crossed her arms in front of her. "Um, okay, what does that even mean?" She was genuinely curious. She wanted to wrap her head around it.

"The hosts organize these naked pool parties. I mean, clothing optional. Everyone starts off in swimsuits but after a few drinks, the clothes come off. And after a few more drinks, some people start touching each other, of course. And some of them end up having sex."

"Like, out in the open?" Sally repeated, incredulous.

"Yeah, on big lounge beds around the pool."

"Some of them? What's everyone else doing while they are having sex out in the open?"

"Some watch and some don't pay much attention and just carry on with whatever they're doing, swimming, talking, you know."

No, she did not know. Sally had never imagined such a scene

occurring in real life. That was a porn plot, not a suburban pool party.

"I take it that those people were definitely not vanilla?"

Kate laughed. "Definitely not."

Sally wondered how "vanilla" Kate had been at that party, and how passive her role had actually been. She was afraid to ask because she wasn't sure she really wanted to know how far her sister had gone, or would go, in that situation. She did want to know more about the sex out in the open thing, though. "So was it like group sex, or couples?"

"Both, I guess. I mean, there were several combinations. But the interesting thing was, as I said, that I was shocked at first, but then I liked it. It was really hot, watching people like that." Kate's gaze turned to somewhere over Sally's shoulder, but her eyes seemed to glaze over for a second. She shook her head and snapped back to reality. "Anyway, that's my secret."

Kate clearly wanted to leave it at that and change the subject, which meant there was far more to the story. She could squirm, for once.

"So you just watched?"

Kate didn't flinch. "Yes, I just watched. I wasn't going to just jump in. It was the first time I'd ever seen anything like that."

"Oh, the first time, eh? The first of many?"

"Oh, stop it! That's enough secrets for now. I don't want you going home thinking about me at naked pool parties. Go home thinking about that handsome surfer dude and his hot redhead."

Kate had a point. Even though hearing about her sister's wild side was fun, it was better not to taint her fantasies with images of her at nude pool parties. Parties, she had said. Plural. Did that mean she had been to more than one? That question would have to wait for another day and another bottle of wine.

"Or better yet, I can go home and think about my handsome husband."

"Or, sure, think about your husband. Good luck with that one, though. After all this, I think you will have a hard time only thinking about him now."

"Ha, you might be right." She said "might" but Sally knew her sister was spot on.

CHAPTER 7

Sally still had a wine buzz when she got home just after three. Shane would be home by five. She arranged the two-dozen red roses she had picked up on the way home in a big vase and sat them on her bedside table. She fiddled with the candles on the dresser and bedside table, not sure what do with herself for the hour and a half before Shane returned.

Maybe she should take a bath to freshen up. She could shave her legs so they would be as smooth as her freshly waxed pussy. The scent of the lavender bubble bath flooded the room with sweetness while Sally undressed and waited for the tub to fill.

She studied herself in the mirror while she undressed. Sally rubbed her hands over her breasts. Naughty girl. They were firm under her touch. She slid the pink panties off and admired the new look of her pussy. Thankfully the redness had greatly improved. She smiled at the form in the mirror. Not bad for nearly thirty-three.

Why was it that she never wore anything that accented her sexy body? Almost never. Excitement stirred in her belly. She couldn't wait to model the new underwear for Shane.

Sally brought a candle from beside the bed and lit it before she slipped into the tub to soak. The bubbles tickled her breasts as she laid back onto the inflatable shell-shaped pillow and breathed in the sweet scent. Slick from the bubbles, Sally rubbed her arms, then her legs. They were prickly with stubble. The bubbles were too deep to try to shave. She'd just have to relax for a while to let them die down.

Her hands slid over her breasts again; she lingered and made circles around her nipples. When Sally closed her eyes the images returned. The contrast of the redhead's pink nipples with her milky white skin. The smooth pussy. The long, hard cock. Her own hardened nipples tingled under her touch. Sally slid a hand over her flat belly to her pussy. The smoothness extended all the way back to between her cheeks. It felt amazing.

Sally's clit throbbed, craving her touch. The nub hardened and swelled from under its hood when she drew circles around the base. She started to rub the crest of the bean with the tips of two fingers, but it was too much. She slipped the fingers inside instead and played with her nipple with the other hand. Sally clenched around her fingers; in and out, in and out. When she returned to the clit, she took it slow, first around the base and then gently sliding over the gem. Electric pulses moved out from the epicenter in waves. She was on a cliff, ready to fly but afraid to jump.

Sally stopped, then started again, repeatedly taking herself to the edge, ready to scream, then backing off. Prolonging the orgasm made the desire for it greater. She could see the hot couple from the library clear as day through her closed eyes. His cock, so long and thick, thrusting into the redhead's slick and swollen pussy. Then that cock was in her, in Sally, stretching her out, filling her up. His mouth on her nipple, sucking and nibbling.

The orgasm welled up inside her like a tidal wave. Sally twirled her nipple between the fingers of the other hand while she massaged her clit. She squirmed under her own touch, making waves in the tub with her thrashing until she heard herself moaning in the candlelight. She drove the fingers inside and squeezed her warm, smooth walls around them in rhythm with the waves inside until they receded and she went limp.

When had she masturbated twice in a 24-hour period? Ever? Come to think of it, she couldn't actually remember when she had last masturbated prior to the library peep show. It just wasn't something she did, normally. She didn't need to please herself. She had a husband for that. Anytime she felt horny, all she ever had to do was kiss Shane on the neck and stroke his package, and he would happily take care of all her needs. He knew how to get the job done, every time. It was simple and easy. Predictable but reliable. It had always been all that she needed.

Sally felt different since seeing the couple in the library, though. Her desires were rawer, more intense. More immediate. She *had* to masturbate because she had to have it *right then*. Her orgasms were different, too. Better? Maybe. A knot tightened in her stomach and pushed up into her throat. Guilt. Guilt diluted with bliss. Or was it the other way around?

Sally shaved her legs smooth and hoisted herself up out of the tub, her limbs as loose as noodles after the intense orgasm and the long soak. There was nothing to feel guilty about. She was just gearing up for a sexy afternoon with her husband. It was all perfectly normal, and perfectly innocent. Sally laughed out loud. None of this was normal for her, and thinking about another guy's cock inside her while masturbating in the tub didn't feel so innocent. She toweled off and slipped into her pink satin robe. It was a quarter past four, still half an hour or more until Shane would be home. Sally's eyelids felt as heavy as her limbs. Maybe she had time for a quick nap. On second thought, Shane finding her drooling on her pillow was not the romantic prelude to the afternoon of hot sex she had imagined. She'd better keep moving. She could get herself and the bedroom ready for the escapades ahead.

A bottle of champagne had been in the bottom of the fridge since New Year's Eve. Perfect. Sally placed it in an ice bucket on the night table with two glasses, alongside the bouquet of roses. She pulled the head off one of the roses and scattered the petals along the bottom of the bed. It looked like a movie scene. Now to dress the leading lady.

The lingerie felt silky when she rubbed it on her cheek again. The fabric had a plasticky new smell that wasn't exactly appealing. She squirted it with her favorite perfume, appropriately called Desire. Sally easily slipped the semi-thong underwear over her bath-oiled skin. The heart-like crests accented her muscular ass beautifully. Why was it that she never wore thongs? They weren't uncomfortable like she had once imagined they'd be, and they were sexy as hell. She always defaulted to practical. Her gynecologist once told her that cotton briefs let her lady bits breathe best, so that's what she'd always used. She had been missing out.

Sally let her hair down and sat to brush it in front of the mirror. A few curls would be nice. She plugged in her curling iron and opened her cosmetic bag. How strange it was to put on makeup to go to bed. She laughed as she added pink rouge to her cheeks. She barely even wore makeup to work, and only a little more when they went out at night. But this was a special occasion and warranted the full face, complete with shimmering eye shadow and lipstick. Her red lips made the red ribbon on the bra stand out. A few soft curls around her face were all she needed to perfect the look. A hot blonde, looking more like a high-priced call girl than a librarian, stared back from the other side of the glass. Who was that woman?

It was ten to five by the time Sally finished her hair and make up. Shane would be home any minute. She rushed to pull the shades and light a few candles around the room and positioned herself to wait on the bed. She sat in a suggestive pose with her knees bent and over to one side. But maybe should she be lying down. No, sitting up was better. The knot tightened in her stomach again. Nervous energy.

Perfume! Sally had squirted the lingerie but not herself. It was Shane's favorite scent. She rushed back to the bathroom and pumped Desire on each of her wrists, which she rubbed behind her ears, another that she rubbed between her thighs, and one last pump on her belly. On her way back to the bed she heard the garage door opening.

Sally leapt onto the bed and back into position. Then the bottom fell out of her stomach, into the pit of doubt. Shit, she looked like a prostitute! What was she thinking? Shane would think she had lost her mind. She should cover up at least, to ease into it. Sally's heart raced as she bolted back to the bathroom to grab her robe. She tied it on while running full speed back to the bed, and jumped onto the bed, lying down just in time to hear Shane calling her name as he made his way through the house. She was a perfectly wrapped pink satin present, complete with bow.

CHAPTER 8

Heat rose to Sally's cheeks as Shane called for her. She stayed quiet. He would have to find her.

Shane stopped in this tracks in the bedroom doorway and eyed Sally suspiciously. Her face strained to hold the big fake grin that she hoped hid the fear that bubbled up into her throat. Her chest heaved up and down like she was hyperventilating. This had all been a terrible idea. He would think she was playing some role, or that she was crazy. Because this, this, could not be Sally. He would know it. He knew her. And he was right. This was not her. Who was she trying to be?

Sally searched his face for clues. If he rejected her, she would just die. She would find a cave, crawl into it, and die.

Shane surveyed the scene. From the dark rose petals on the white bedspread to the candles lining the bedside tables to Sally, a flower herself, a pink bloom adorned with brushes of colors and curls.

Sally's tension eased a bit when Shane smiled and shook his head as he approached the edge of the bed.

"Wow, I guess your leader granted my request and let you stay."

Sally was afraid she might vomit if she unclenched her teeth to speak, but she did anyway. "Yes, permission was granted." Her attempt at mimicking a robotic sort of voice ended up sounding silly.

"Well, thank goodness for that." Shane sat beside Sally. "You look great." He leaned in close to her neck. "Oh wow, you smell great, too."

Shane's warm breath on her neck stirred a warmth between Sally's legs. The prickling sensation of hairs standing spread up her arms. Sally drew a deep breath. She could do this. She wasn't playing someone else. She was playing the real Sally. She pulled him by the necktie so that their lips we nearly touching. "See how I taste."

Shane wrapped his arms around her and swallowed her up in an embrace as deep as the kiss. There was definitely a lot more tongue and a lot more passion involved than their usual kisses. Tingling brewed in her crotch as her hands moved up and down Shane's muscular back. She pulled his shirttails from his pants and slipped her hands underneath to feel his warm, soft skin over his hard body. Sally nearly choked on his tongue pushing deeper into her throat when she pulled Shane over her. His heaviness and his broad shoulders pinned her underneath him. Trapped. There was no place she would rather be.

Shane's cock pressed through his pants into Sally's thigh. The tingling in her crotch intensified. She couldn't wait to have that big, hard dick inside her. Moisture spread into her new black lace panties. When Sally closed her eyes, she saw the surfer dude thrusting into the pretty girl the night before. She didn't want to think it; it was just there. The knot in her stomach returned. The guilt again. Sally opened her eyes to try to shake the image but the hot surfer dude was there with them, his cock superimposed on Shane, pieces of their features mixing. She was just going to have to accept it. He was there with them. And that thought was all it took to take her to the edge. She could come in a second, and they had only just begun.

Sally moaned as she dry humped the bulge pressing through Shane's pants. Shane traced the line of her jaw from her ear to her chin and studied her face while she moaned. He placed his hand on her chest and left it there. He wasn't responding to her grinding. Dread spread from deep in her gut upward when Sally tried to bite his ear but he stopped her. This was it. Rejection.

"What has gotten into you, babe? I mean, don't get me wrong. I am not complaining, at all, but I have to wonder." Shane's eyes changed to a look of mock suspicion as he wrinkled his brow. "Did they really replace you with a horny alien?" He giggled.

Oh, thank God. He was joking. There was still hope. Sally laughed and pulled his mouth back to hers for a kiss. "Maybe they did. Would you be sad if the old Sally was gone forever?"

Shane's brow wrinkled again. "I feel like that is a Catch 22 question. There is no right answer. Unless, of course, you are the alien replacement, in which case my answer would be 'No, that would be fine with me.'" He kissed her again.

"Good." Sally shifted to try to flip Shane over. He cooperated and rolled onto his back so that she could climb on top of him. Sally straddled him and loosened his necktie, then unbuttoned his dress shirt to expose his chiseled chest. She had loved those muscles since college. She traced the line of his nipple on his pecs. The wetness in her crotch spread further as she ran her fingers down to the button of his slacks. His hardened cock pulsed under her, pressing into her moist mound through the robe and the lingerie. Shane's piercing aquamarine eyes stared right into her soul. He could see that she was no imposter.

Those eyes had been what hooked Sally; she was so easily lost in them. Caribbean blue and framed by long black lashes and thick, dark brows, they were his defining feature from birth. His mother bragged that strangers would stop her to tell her how smitten they were with him and his eyes when he was a toddler. Of course, it helped that the eyes were set in an incredibly handsome face, defined by a square jaw and full lips, and a narrow, straight nose. Shane was the cutest guy Sally had ever dated. In fact, she didn't usually like guys that were *that* good looking, because they were usually jerks. Not Shane, though. He was sweet as could be, and salt of the earth. It was probably because he was so smart, and had been a geek through adolescence, that he never developed the cocky disposition typical of really hot guys. They had hit it off right away, and despite his good looks, Sally could see that he was a genuinely good guy.

Sally unfastened Shane's belt and unbuttoned his pants. Warmth gushed into her panties again with the sight of the smooth head of his cock peeking out over his boxers. It begged for a kiss. Shane gasped as Sally moved down to suck him. He ran his hands through her blonde curls and over her shoulders, covered by the silky robe, while she took him deep into her mouth. Sally swallowed him up, as deep as she could, for at least a couple of minutes, then pulled back to give herself a break from the deep throat action, licking up and down Shane's long shaft. Sally never minded giving oral sex, and she certainly loved receiving it, but she was enjoying sucking Shane's cock more than ever before. When she tried to put the whole thing in her mouth again, Shane pulled her up to him.

"What's the matter, don't you like it?"

"Oh, I like it. I like it too much. You're gonna make me come, and it's too soon for that." He pulled her into another deep kiss, and Sally extended her legs so that she laid atop him. She remembered the blonde hunk pulling the redhead up to him after stopping her from sucking his cock. The electricity in her crotch intensified. She pressed her pelvis into Shane, grinding her pubic bone into his hard shaft as they kissed. Sally forced her eyes open, to see Shane, because when she closed them he became the hot blonde surfer dude in her mind's eye.

Shane rolled Sally over off him to the center of the bed and got up to undress. He dropped his trousers and boxers first, then loosened his tie and started to unbutton his shirt. He looked so hot standing there, in his open shirt and tie, admiring her from the side of the bed. How lucky was she that she gets to fuck this guy for the rest of her life? Pretty damn lucky. She didn't need, or even really want, another, even if her mind wandered there.

Shane's eyes locked hers as he sat on the bed beside her, and they held her gaze while he slowly and deliberately untied the belt of her robe, unwrapping his gift. Butterflies spiraled upward from Sally's belly to her throat anticipating his reaction to the lingerie. Shane's blue eyes widened as they moved up, then down, then back up her body again.

"Wow, what is this?" A tickle stirred as he traced the red ribbon trim along the edge of her breast, then brushed her nipple through the lace with the back of his finger.

"I saw it in the store window after my pedicure this morning. I thought you might like it."

"You thought right." Shane climbed back over her and kissed Sally's neck, inhaling her scent while he ran his tongue up to lick and nibble her earlobe. "What a nice surprise. We should do this more often."

"Yes, we really should."

It was difficult to catch her breath when Shane caressed her breast. When he pulled the bra down to lick and kiss and suck her hard pink nipple, Sally moaned in delight. Her moans grew deeper when Shane moved his hand between her legs. Sally pushed her hips up into his hand, her wetness seeping through the lace. She dug her nails into his back. "Oh yeah, just like that."

Sally wrapped her fingers around Shane's cock and massaged the shaft while he moved back to her neck to kiss her. "You're so hard. I've never seen you like this."

"And you're so wet. So wet." Shane slipped his hand inside the black lace underwear. His hand felt rough on the new smoothness of Sally's pussy. Shane's hard breathing stopped along with his hand, still inside her panties. "Whoa, what's this?" He stood on his knees and gaped at her crotch as he pulled the new underwear down to her knees. His eyes widened at her exposed, freshly waxed pussy. "Holy shit, babe, that is hot!"

"Oh, I guess I didn't mention that I also got a new style down there."

Shane's mouth dropped open as he stared. "Well, I'd say."

Sally wiggled her knees to push the panties all the way down, then kicked the underwear off her foot. "I thought you might like a change."

"Well change you have. I was joking before, but now I'm seriously wondering if you've been kidnapped and replaced." Shane stretched his legs out and laid beside her, then brushed a curl behind her ear.

"You look like you." He leaned in to kiss her neck and inhaled deeply, his mouth just behind her ear.

"You smell like you." He sucked her earlobe.

"You taste like you." He rubbed the nearly hairless mound between her legs.

"But you don't feel like you, not down there." Shane's smile faded as he searched her eyes for answers while confusion set into his.

CHAPTER 9

Shane's erection wilted in her hand. Sally gripped him to try to dam up the escaping passion. "It's okay, babe. Of course, it's me." Her voice cracked. "I thought you'd like it. Is it too weird?" Sally resisted the urge to cover herself, so exposed in just her black lace bra with the red ribbon trim.

Shane focused on her crotch before meeting her eyes. "No, it's not too weird. I mean, you getting waxed is not *that* weird. Or, well, it wouldn't be, except it *is* that weird for you. Since when would you ever think to do this? I've known you over ten years and I don't remember even a mention of you considering something like this."

Sally kept her voice as calm and even as possible, despite the doubt welling up in her gut. "Well in that same amount of time, I don't recall you over mentioning that you might like me to do something like this either. But you do, don't you?" She stroked his nearly flaccid shaft, attempting resuscitation.

"I guess that's true. But why this, why now, Sal?" The faint tremble in his voice hinted a tinge of sadness, or was it fear?

Sally traced a line from his chest to his pubic hair. "Why ask why, babe, let's just enjoy this moment. I want you. You want me. And this connection, it's good for us."

"Babe, believe me, I want to fuck your brains out. I mean, look at you." His gaze surveyed her head to toe. His cock twitched ever so slightly. There was hope. "But I need to know: Are you okay? I mean, is anything wrong?"

Sally straddled him and sat back on her heels, her moist crotch pressing into his softened package. "I want to fuck your brains out, too. And, no, there's nothing wrong. In fact, everything feels right." She moved her hips to grind into him. "I had a little epiphany today, I guess." She leaned in for a long kiss.

Shane pulled away from her kiss and grinned. "Oh yeah, what was that? The waxed pussy epiphany?" His smirk was so sexy. Signs of life returned to his penis, but it was still severely deflated.

"Ha, well, yeah, eventually. But it came from something, an awakening, I suppose." Sally moved her hips to press into his dick and held it there while she continued. "I realized that I have been so guarded all my life, so afraid to let loose and really be me. Life is too short for that. Right now I feel truly connected to my sexual energy for the first time ever. And I want to share that with you." Sally pushed her pubis harder into his stiffening cock and leaned in for another kiss.

Shane relaxed into her kiss and grew hard again under Sally's grinding pelvis. She slid her slick slit up and down his shaft until it was rock hard, then guided him between her wet lips, but not yet inside. She rubbed her clit along his stiff shaft, then pressed into him while moving her hips side to side.

When her clit was swollen and screaming, Sally squeezed Shane's hips with her knees and pulled him by the shoulders to roll over and flip him on top of her. She moaned, grinding her pelvis into him as he slid up and down, inside her lips but still outside her folds. An emptiness ached inside her. She needed him. Sally guided Shane's pulsing head to her entrance, then gripped the sheets in tight fists and gasped as he filled her up.

With every thrust, Shane penetrated deeper than ever before with his maximum erection, but Sally was so wet that he slid in and out easily. She tightened her grip around him in rhythm with his strokes. Something about the sweat dripping from Shane's chin and landing between her tits, still clad in the black lace bra, caused the contractions deep in her pelvis to intensify. The groans that escaped as Shane pushed to her deepest boundaries were animalistic and unfamiliar.

Shane pulled out and trembled as he buried his face between her breasts. Sally could tell he was trying to control himself, to last longer. She pulled her bra down beneath her breasts, then wiggled to position a breast under Shane's face. Her feet flexed up toward her and her toes splayed as Shane sucked one nipple while twirling the other between his fingertips.

As though he heard her clit screaming for attention, Shane licked a path down her belly to between her legs and parted her moist, swollen lips with his tongue. He rubbed his mouth around the outer lips and moaned, the vibration of his sound reverberating through her. The five o'clock shadow stubble on his chin felt amazing on her smooth lips. Shane stopped moving and drew in a deep breath again. She could tell he was still teetering on the edge of ejaculation. After a couple of deep breaths, he returned his focus to running his tongue around Sally's magic button.

Sally lifted and swirled her hips in circles in rhythm with his kisses, actively seeking his touch, participating in the pursuit of pleasure like never before. Shane moved his hand to feel the solitary line of hair left behind after the waxing, the last remnant of the pussy he remembered. Sally moaned deeper as he slipped two fingers into her wetness while he continued to lick her.

Sally laid back on the pillow and squealed while Shane licked and sucked and nibbled her clit. He knew exactly how to take her to the brink of orgasm, always had. The same familiarity that can make married sex predictable and boring can also make it so damn good. The tingle started at her clit as he rolled his tongue over it, but it spread down her legs and out to her toes, and up to her chest and out to her fingertips. Sally's whole body was electrified. Shock waves started when Shane brushed her nipple with the back of his hand, the rolling thunder of the imminent eruption ignited with his touch.

"Don't stop!" Sally called as she grabbed Shane behind his head, locking him to her crotch.

"Oh, oh, oh my God. Yes, Baby, yeah, Baby, just like that." Her voice climbed three octaves as Sally writhed under the movement of his tongue, pressing her pelvis into his mouth while she gripped his fingers from the inside. Difficult as it was, Shane managed to keep his mouth fixed to her pussy while she bucked like a bull and screamed out in orgasm.

When Sally stopped shivering, Shane moved up to mount her again. His cock stood like a flagpole waiting to be dressed. Sally was drunk with pleasure but had the wherewithal to push Shane away before he entered her again. "Not so fast, Mister. I want to return the favor. That cock is begging to be sucked."

Sally rolled him over and kissed her way down Shane's belly. "Just relax, babe, you deserve it."

She tucked her lips around her teeth and applied a steady pressure as she swallowed his hard cock. You'd think Sally had pleasure sensors in her throat the way she moaned while she sucked him. She tried a new trick, stroking and gently squeezing Shane's balls while she sucked him, just like the redhead did the night before in the library.

Shane moaned but then pulled back and guided Sally up to his mouth. "Wait, babe, I am trying hard to last."

Sally wrapped her hand around Shane's engorged shaft. "You're certainly hard, alright."

He kept his eye fixed on hers while he peeled her fingers off his cock and bent forward to back his pelvis away from her. "Seriously, you gotta stop for a minute."

Shane slid his hands behind her back to unclasp her bra as he kissed her mouth. He cupped Sally's breasts. "You have the best tits, you know that?"

"I'm glad you appreciate them."

"They're fucking amazing. Women pay to have tits like these." Shane kissed her as he sat up, and used the hold on her boobs to guide her back onto her back, squeezing her breasts hard enough to hurt just a little. Shane moved one hand back down toward her crotch and brushed the tiny patch of hair above her slit. "And this pussy. Wow. I have always loved your pussy. But I have never seen it quite like this."

"Yeah, well no one has ever seen it quite like the lady who did this to me did."

Shane laughed as he slid his hand back between her legs. Sally knew she was ripe for another orgasm because Shane's touch immediately stirred the electric warmth that quickly spread from her crotch down to her toes. She moved her hips under his touch as he moved his mouth to her breast, nibbling and sucking her nipple while he slipped two fingers into her. Sally made circles with her pelvis to grind her clit into Shane's palm. His gentle nibbling of her nipple, and his fingers inside her hooking forward toward her pubic bone while her clit rubbed his palm, created the trifecta of stimulation. Within seconds, Sally was writhing again in climax and screaming his name. Sally hadn't had multiple orgasms for as long as either of them could remember.

After Sally finished, Shane kissed his way back up to her mouth and threw a leg over her. Sally's chest heaved up and down under him. She could barely breathe. "You know, you're the best thing that ever happened to me, you sexy man."

Shane guided the tip of his dick around her moist opening, exploring the feel of the unfamiliar pussy. "Babe, you are so fucking hot. Holy shit, I just can't believe you," he whispered into her ear, teasing her with the head of his dick just inside her.

"Yes, fuck me, Baby, fuck me," Sally commanded as she lifted her hips to thrust herself onto him. Aggressive and demanding was a role she rarely inhabited in their sex life. She pulled him from his buttocks as Shane pushed his cock into her slick opening and deep into her. "Yeah, like that," Sally encouraged as he thrust in and out of her. She laid back and let Shane drill her. "Just like that, fuck me, harder, Baby, harder."

Shane pushed deeper into her and moved one hand over her breasts. He pinched and twirled her nipples as he pounded into her.

Sally encouraged him to keep up the pace. "Yeah, Baby, you know how to fuck me. Go faster, faster!"

The image of the surfer drilling his girlfriend the night before returned. As Shane fucked her, Sally was transported back to that moment, watching from the end of the aisle, so turned on, waiting for their finish. She gripped tight from the inside to clutch Shane's penis as it thrust in and out of her. When Shane started to moan in his climax, she, too, erupted into an unexpected third orgasm. The grip around his cock became rhythmic and involuntary; she pulsed around him as he pumped into her, both of them grunting and groaning like primal creatures. It was the first orgasm she had ever had without direct clitoral stimulation in her thirty-two-and-a-half years.

Shane collapsed onto her, sweaty and breathless after the simultaneous orgasm. After a minute or so, Sally struggled to speak under Shane's weight.

"I guess you like the new hairdo."

Shane could barely move, let alone speak, at that point, so he did not voice all the questions that were likely already swirling in his head. "Yeah, it's amazing," was all he could muster.

Sally pushed Shane up to unweight her so she could speak. "We have champagne!" She was suddenly energized and as bubbly as the beverage she was suggesting.

Shane looked over to the chilled bottle and two champagne flutes beside the bed. “You thought of everything, didn’t you?” He studied his wife through half-opened eyes with curious awe.

Shane slid himself out of her and shifted to grab the champagne off the table.

“I didn’t even think of the time of the month.” Shane momentarily snapped back to reality and worried about their lack of birth control.

“It’s okay, I did. I should be at least four days from ovulation.” Sally hoped her cycle was as regular that month as it usually was. Normally, they were careful to use condoms in the week that she might be ovulating. Technically she was within the danger zone, but under the circumstances, it seemed worth the risk for the sake of spontaneity.

“Four days sounds like cutting it kind of close, babe.” Shane’s brow wrinkled with worry while he poured the bubbly.

CHAPTER 10

Sally leaned back against Shane's chest as they sipped champagne naked in the bed. Nearing the end of his first glass, Shane finally got the nerve to ask Sally about her apparent vaginal orgasm. "So at the end there, did you come, too?"

Sally raised up and turned to face him, her eyes twinkling with a smile."Yeah, I did."

Shane traced circles around her breasts, still tingling. "Wow, that's a first." He grinned like a teenager after his first time. It felt like their first time, in a way.

"Actually it was a third, but technically, you're right, it was a first." Sally gulped the last of her champagne. Five orgasms in less than twenty-four hours, a record by a long shot.

Sally poured them both another glass. Shane was so hot, so handsome, laying back on the pillow studying her. She kissed him as she handed him the glass. "I hope you liked your surprise."

"Well, I'm certainly surprised."

Sally grinned and settled into the nook of his arm, propped up on pillows. "I know it must have seemed weird, but I'm glad you could just relax and go with it. I needed this. *We* needed this."

Acknowledging the weirdness of it all seemed to open the floodgates of Shane's doubts. He stiffened under Sally. "So, babe, now you have to tell me, what gives? Since we woke up today, you have been acting very strange." He shifted uncomfortably in the bed. "First, you nearly attacked me in the morning, which was nice, very nice, but also highly unusual." He sipped his champagne and cleared his throat. "And then, you go buy lingerie and get yourself waxed, two things I have never known you to do in over ten years. And then, you stage this amazing afternoon, which I loved, but, once again, is highly unusual." He stroked her shoulder gently. "So I know something is going on. The question is, what? Please tell me." He sipped his champagne again then drew in another deep breath. "Honestly, babe, is this about your biological clock?"

"What? No!" Sally hadn't meant to nearly shout. She laughed at the suggestion as she turned to face Shane. "God no. We've long established that, haven't we? No kids, no way."

"Well, yeah, but there are hormones, Mother Nature, propagation of the species, and all that, well, biology. They say that all women eventually feel the need to have children. I didn't think so in your case, after all that we have talked about. But I have always wondered if it may change for you at some point. The biological clock might not be a myth." Shane sounded almost smug in his assessment. He was so far off the mark.

Sally wanted to laugh in his face, but she took a deep breath so she could answer calmly instead. "The only clock I hear ticking is the big one, the life clock. Life is short. We only live once, so we might as well enjoy it to the fullest." Her voice and manner softened as she stroked his thigh. "Right, babe?"

Shane watched Sally with slanted eyes. He wasn't really buying it, she could tell. And who could blame him? Nothing had yet explained how he woke up with a drastically different wife today. "Well, that sounds vague, and, again, not at all like you."

Sally was not sure how to explain herself. "Babe, like I said, I just got a whiff of what our life could be like, what it should be like. It occurred to me that we've been living our life at half-intensity, happily but with the volume set at five. I guess I just realized that if we dared to turn it up a little, we might like it a lot more."

Shane's brow wrinkled as he sipped his champagne. "Okay, but why? What sparked this realization?" There was a notable tinge of sarcasm when he said 'realization'. Was he mocking her?

"Well, it might sound weird." Sally bit her lip while contemplating whether she wanted to tell him about her experience the night before. She didn't really see any other option since he was getting suspicious, and perhaps even hurt, over the change he saw in her.

"Try me," Shane encouraged, resting his hand on her knee.

"It's really embarrassing to say it out loud, but last night in the library I saw something that really affected me." Sally hesitated, doubting whether she could continue.

"In the *library*?" Shane's face contorted into a strange

combination of confusion and on the verge of bursting out laughing.

"Yeah, at the end of the night, I happened upon a couple. They were, um, messing around." Heat rushed to Sally's face. You'd think she was the one caught with her pants down.

"Okay," Shane's face softened as he encouraged her to continue. "So, they were making out?"

Sally drew in another deep breath. Just spit it out. "Yeah, big time. And they didn't see me, so I stayed, watching." Even though there was no one around to hear, Sally subconsciously lowered her voice to nearly a whisper to continue. "I saw them have sex." A lump formed; her throat closed. She couldn't look at Shane, too afraid of what his face might tell her, of what he might be thinking of her. He didn't say a word. Sally's voice trembled as she forced herself to continue. "It was the biggest turn on." She felt the tension start to leave her body immediately upon the admission, still embarrassed but also relieved to share the secret. It wasn't the watching that made her feel naughty and ashamed, it was the liking it.

Sally lifted her eyes to Shane. He laid back staring up at the ceiling. She knew the look of his wheels turning as he tried to process it all. "So you watched them have sex?" His gaze met hers. "In the *library*?" His voice carried the undertones of his predominant thought: *What the fuck?*

"Yes, and afterward I couldn't think about anything else." Sally was naked and exposed, vulnerable but liberated. She crossed her ankles and drew her knees in close, sipping her champagne as she watched her husband drink his.

Shane seemed thoughtful for a moment before he responded. "So seeing college kids fucking turned you on so much that you went out and bought lingerie and got your privates waxed?"

The wording of Shane's response was so reserved that Sally knew they were made for one another. Her privates. She would have giggled had she not been so nervous and embarrassed. Wondering what he must be thinking of her was almost painful. The undertones of his question told her that he didn't really understand the connection between her accidental voyeurism and her radical transformation literally from one day to the next.

"I guess so." It did sound a bit far-fetched. Shane watched her with a discerning stare. He was obviously having a hard time swallowing it.

Sally filled both their glasses again. They were really downing the bubbly. She hoped it might help her to explain, or him to understand. "I know it sounds sort of crazy. But when I was hiding there, watching them have sex, I felt incredibly aroused. I knew I should just turn and get lost, but I couldn't. I loved seeing it. They were so into one another, and they were both so hot. I just couldn't leave."

Shane sipped his champagne and took a deep breath. "Okay, so you watched them have sex. Then what? I mean, why is that life-altering?" His sarcastic tone felt like mocking and stabbed like a dagger.

"I don't know!" Sally drew her knees in toward her chest to cover herself then wrapped her arms around her knees to make herself as small as possible. "Are you *trying* to make me feel like a freak now? Because I do. I can't explain what happened to me there. But it did." She was defensive. Maybe telling him had been a mistake. Maybe he wasn't ready for that. Maybe she wasn't either.

Shane's face softened as he rested his hand on her knee. "No, I don't mean to make you feel like a freak. I am just trying to understand what came over you, babe. And to be honest, it's kind of hard to believe."

Sally had to try to explain herself, whether she wanted to or not. "Well, hard as it may be to believe, that's what happened. And after watching them, I was charged with a crazy energy. It's hard to explain. I literally couldn't think about *anything* else. I came home super horny last night, but you were in bed. I wanted to wake you up. I wanted to tell you. And I wanted to fuck you. I thought you'd think I was crazy, though, so I masturbated in the tub. It was the first time I have done that in God knows how long." She paused to sip again. She knew she was babbling, but it just all came out.

Shane was quiet, too quiet. Sally shifted nervously and took another big gulp of bubbly. "What is it, babe?"

Shane inhaled deeply and held his breath for second before answering. "I am just trying to process this. Trying to understand this. Trying to believe this."

Sally tried to decipher the messages of doubt. Granted, happening upon a sexy couple having sex in public wasn't your everyday occurrence, but it was not beyond the realm of possibilities, was it? Or was it that she was so profoundly affected by the sight that was so hard to believe?

"I guess that's why I woke up thinking about sex again this morning, and why I came onto you before work. I was still charged with that energy." Sally tried to read Shane's face but his steady stare and hardened brow weren't giving anything away.

"I hadn't planned to get the waxing, but there was a special in the salon when I went for my pedicure. I decided to try it because I thought that woman's smooth pussy looked so hot last night." She paused to inhale. She was rambling again.

Shane's jaw dropped at his wife's last words. His face said *What the fuck?* "Really? You thought another woman's pussy was hot?" The corners of his mouth curled into a wry smile.

Sally downed the rest of her champagne. "Yes, really. I mean, I thought the whole scene was really hot, including her Brazilian-waxed pussy." She summoned the strength to continue. "And the reason I got the lingerie was that I thought I'd look so hot in it that you wouldn't be able to resist me, so you would have to ravage me."

"You mean I'd be like he was with her, last night in the library?" Shane's eyebrows lifted. Maybe he was starting to understand. It sounded like he may even be getting into the fantasy.

The edge in Shane's voice had softened. He was almost flirty. Sally let herself believe it was okay. "Yeah, I guess so." She smiled back at him. "It was incredibly hot, babe."

Shane looked at her with wonder and ran his finger up the back of Sally's thigh toward her knees that were still hugged tight into her chest.

"So you enjoyed seeing them so much that you did all this?"

"Well, I think it's better to say that I enjoyed seeing them so much that it sparked a desire in me like none I've ever felt."

"Whoa, that's intense," Shane said, his blue eyes staring directly into hers. "Ever?" he asked.

CHAPTER 11

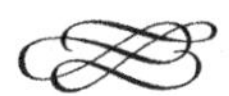

Sally studied Shane's face. Maybe he felt threatened? She definitely didn't want that.

"Today I realized that even though everything has always been good, and I've never had any reason to complain, maybe it could be so much better if I could somehow just let go and let it happen. And I don't mean just sex. I mean everything. That's why I said that we can turn the volume up, and enjoy it so much more. The intensity of what I experienced made me think that. Life shouldn't be lived at five when ten can be so much more fun!"

Shane ran his fingers through his dark hair. He looked to be contemplating Sally's euphoria.

"Have you, by chance, talked to Kate about this?" Shane couldn't mask the smirk that spread across his face.

"Um, yes, actually. I had lunch with her today. Why?" Sally's eyes narrowed. What was he trying to say, exactly?

Shane chuckled. "Oh really? Did she give you some special brownies for dessert?"

"Ha! Me? Yeah, right! But we did have a little wine." It dawned on her what Shane had implied. "Why? Do you think I sound stoned?" She didn't really like where this was going.

"No, you just sound a lot more like your sister than yourself. You know, 'YOLO' and 'Live life at a ten.' That's Kate, not you, babe."

"Well, maybe Kate has been right all along." Sally was beyond defensive. Not only was Shane making fun of her, he was trying to insult her by comparing her to her sister, which just pissed her off. She could insult her sister if and when she chose, but no one else better do it.

"You know, I don't appreciate that, not in the least. First of all, Kate had nothing to do with what is going on with me. I called her to tell her about buying the lingerie and she asked me to have lunch. Yes, I told her about what I saw last night, but I was already feeling this way. And second, it's really not nice of you to imply that my sounding like my sister is a bad thing. I know she's quirky, but I love her. And sometimes I wish I could be more like her."

Shane apparently picked up on Sally's prickliness and decided to take it down a notch. "I'm sorry, babe. I didn't mean it like that. I love Kate, too. I'm just trying to understand what happened with you."

Shane oozed sincerity, from his voice, from his eyes, from his gentle touch as he stroked Sally's thigh in the space just below her butt cheek, where her foot was tucked as she sat with her knees under her chin. She was overcome with wanting again. She set her glass on the bedside table so that she could attack him.

Sally wrapped her arms around Shane's neck and kissed him hungrily. Even though she had taken him by surprise, Shane accepted her tongue and kissed her back just as hard. He held his champagne glass up in the air and pulled her into him with his one free hand around her waist. Sally kissed her way over to his ear and licked and nibbled at the lobe.

Sally whispered in his ear with heavy breath, "I just want to fuck you, babe. And I want to keep wanting to fuck you this much, forever. It's the most amazing thing I've ever felt, wanting you so much. I need you. I need your touch, I need you inside me." Sally kissed down his neck while feeling for his cock. He was already getting hard. She stroked the length of his shaft, then took hold of it, making a loop around it with her forefinger and thumb, and worked it up and down. Sally got wet feeling him grow in her hand, her pussy almost dripping.

When Shane was fully erect, Sally took the swollen head of his thick cock into her mouth and licked around the base of it, tickling it with her tongue while she continued to jerk him off. Shane gasped to catch his breath, and nearly spilled his champagne on himself as he shuddered. He put his glass on the table and grabbed Sally's hair with both hands, driving his cock deeper into her throat. Sally took it, swallowing up his length deeper than she ever had before. She massaged his balls with the palm of her hand while moving up and down as on his long, thick dick, as fast as she could.

Shane threw his head back and cried up to the ceiling. "Oh Baby, oh Baby, I can't believe you're gonna make me come again."

Sally lifted her mouth off him and strangled the base of his cock with one hand while pressing on the bridge between his ass and his dick with the other, to try to stop the flow. "Oh no you don't, mister. I want you inside me again," she commanded. Sally felt the pulsing under the pressure of her fingers.

Shane choked back the orgasm that brewed and stared at Sally like he didn't recognize her. He held his breath trying to hold back the ejaculation. Sally kept a steady pressure with both hands, but no movement. She tried to catch her breath while staring him in the eye. The way he eyed her said that he still couldn't quite believe what was happening. She liked that. She was surprising, unpredictable.

After a several seconds, Shane exhaled and pulled her up gently to guide her to ride him. Sally straddled him and lowered herself onto his engorged rod. She couldn't help but squeal as it slid into her, filling her up. She clenched tight to feel him pulsing inside her. Shane cupped a breast with one hand and placed the other just above his cock with the palm facing upward so that he could hook into the nook of Sally's clit with two fingers. He was all in. Sally could feel him to the limit of her depths while she moved forward and backward, grinding her clit into his fingertips.

"Oh God, Shane, now you're going to make me come again," Sally squealed. She rode him hard, grinding faster and faster while the tingling built until it exploded in a guttural scream.

Shane watched Sally throw back her head and arch her back as she called up to the sky in ecstasy. She sounded like a wild animal and acted more like one than she ever had before today. He pinched and flicked her nipple while she came, making her scream even louder. Focusing on Sally's orgasm helped Shane forget about trying not to come himself. He was still going strong. He let her finish her orgasm but soon after she collapsed on his chest, Shane roused her by stroking her breast, then twisting her nipple. Sally lifted her head to meet Shane's mischievous gaze. "Harder." She bit her lip and kept her eyes locked with Shane's.

He tightened his grip on her nipple. "So you like to watch?" His stare was intense, captivating, and his hold on her nipple made Sally feel captive, which turned her on immensely.

"Uh huh." Sally started to move her pelvis again, still full with his hardness.

Shane released his grip from her nipple and moved his hands to her hips. He pushed her upward off his stiff cock. "Follow me then."

They stood and he led her across the room to the dresser with its big mirror. Shane stood behind her at the mirror and ran his hands under her arms to cup her breasts. Their eyes locked in the mirror. Shane slid one hand down between Sally's legs and parted her smooth lips so the moist, pink inner parts of her were visible. She watched while Shane used two fingers to pull the hood of her clit back, exposing the tiny pink pearl, her jewel of enormous pleasure. Shane held the hood back with his thumb and ring finger and flicked her clit, already slick with their juices, with the two fingers in between. Sally started to moan immediately and bent forward at the waist to rest her elbows on the dresser, pushing her ass onto Shane's long, hard cock. He rubbed her clit while she pressed into him. Just as her moans turned to screams, he slipped his cock into her wet space. Their eyes locked in the mirror while he fucked her from behind.

Sally arched her back to lift her ass higher to allow Shane to slip even deeper into her. "Yes, fuck me, Baby, fuck me harder, just like that." She lifted her chin as she cooed, like a wolf howling at the moon. Shane stroked the honey-colored curls streaming down her back.

"Harder, harder." Feeling Shane's fingers in her hair while pounding even deeper inside her gave Sally the unusual urge for him to pull her hair a little. She remembered the surfer guy's tight grip at the roots of the woman's red mane the night before. It turns out that Sally didn't need for Shane to actually do it. The fantasy alone, and the returning image of the couple last night, put her over the edge.

Sally felt a pulsing deep in her pelvis and contracted her inner muscles in response, hugging his cock with the slick walls of her pussy. After a few more thrusts, the wave spread like an earthquake from her pelvis upward toward her throat and outward toward her toes. "Oh my God, oh my God. Shaaaannnneee!" Sally caught sight of herself in the mirror as she wailed. She watched her perky tits bounce as Shane's thrusts picked up pace. The chiseled lines of Shane's pectorals and biceps glistened in the candlelight. God, they were sexy. Shane watched her watching him, then leaned in to kiss her neck and ran his tongue up to her ear. "You like to watch me fucking you?" His voice was dripping with desire as he drove himself into her.

"Yes," she swooned. "I love it. I love to watch." Thoughts of the hot couple from the night before flashed through Sally's mind again, causing her to subconsciously tighten her internal grip on Shane's firm cock.

"You naughty girl, I never knew you were such. a. naughty. girl." Shane pounded her harder, for effect, with each of the last four words.

Sally held his gaze in the mirror. "I want to be naughty with you, more naughty. Will you be naughty with me?" She barely recognized herself, pleading with Shane like a submissive schoolgirl. She didn't care how silly she might sound. She was inspired.

Sally's promiscuous persona, combined with her clenching his dick with her tight little pussy, put Shane over the edge. "Fuck yeahhhh." Shane howled as he started to come. He growled like a beast as he lifted Sally's hips so that her feet left the ground while he finished. Sally collapsed onto the dresser, panting, and rested her head on folded arms. Shane continued to move in and out of her, more and more slowly until his erection subsided. He slipped out of her and folded over to rest his chest on Sally's back to catch his breath. Neither of them seemed to care that they were dripping the mixture of sweat and semen all over the floor. At least not until Sensible Sally came to consciousness when she felt it running down her leg, then saw the puddle on the hardwood floor.

"Oh thank God we're not on the rug." She was still out of breath.

Shane laughed then whispered into her ear from behind, "Now I'm sure you're not an imposter. Only my Sally would be equally kinky wild sexy, and concerned about the rug."

Sally looked over her shoulder to answer him. "Ha! I guess that's true. Unless it was a really good imposter. Wait, did you just call me 'kinky wild sexy'?"

Shane kissed the side of her neck and bit into it playfully. "Yes, I did, you horny nymph."

Sally turned and wrapped her arms around his neck, their faces so close they almost touched. "Did you ever think you might consider me a wild, sexy, horny nymph?" Those were not words that either of them, or anyone, would have ever used to describe Sally.

"Nope, but I like it!" Shane pulled her to his mouth and kissed her lips softly.

CHAPTER 12

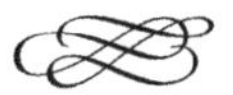

Sally traced circles in Shane's sweaty chest hair. "Well as much as I love being dirty with you, I would really love to get clean with you right now."

"Yeah, I could definitely use a rinse."

Sally led Shane to the shower and washed him with a soapy washcloth as the warm water ran over him. What a sexy man. Her crotch was still pulsing with pleasure. Sally dropped the washcloth and used her hand to lather up his penis and pubic area.

"Don't get any ideas, babe. He's out of commission for a while. You've worn him out."

"Don't worry. I was just playing. I think I fucked myself sore for now, too."

Shane slid a hand between Sally's legs and touched her gently around her outer lips. "Aw, do you need me to kiss it and make it better?"

Sally rubbed her chest against his. “Mmm, that might be nice, but after we eat. I'm famished. How about you?”

“Yes. I definitely worked up an appetite.”

They toweled off then ordered Chinese food and curled up on the bed in their robes to finish off the bottle of champagne while they waited.

Sally rested with her back against Shane’s chest. She heard and felt Shane inhale deeply before he started to speak. Only a strange croak escaped. Sally wrinkled her brow but didn’t move as she tried to make out what was happening with him. She had only heard him choke back tears once, when his grandmother died. It sounded kind of like that.

After a couple of deep breaths, Shane got it together enough to be able to speak. “You know, babe, it’s amazing, I have never felt the way I feel about you right now.”

Butterflies took flight in her stomach. “Oh yeah? How’s that?”

Shane’s voice nearly cracked when he answered. “I love you so fucking much, and I’ve never felt more certain that you are my soul mate.”

Sally's heart swelled upon hearing his voice quiver as Shane professed his love for her. She turned to face him and kissed him softly on the lips. Tears filled his eyes. Shane pulled back to finish. “Look at me, I'm a mess.” His voice cracked, and tears escaped. “It sounds cheesy as hell, I know, but you really take my breath away.” He inhaled deeply again to calm himself. “And I know it's the same love I've always felt for you. But right now, it feels so intense, amplified. Maybe it really is about turning up the volume.”

Sally's eyes teared up. She leaned in to try to kiss Shane but he held her back to continue. "You know the amazing part is not how I'm feeling, though, it's that just an hour or two ago, I was wondering if you were cheating on me and thinking we might be close to over."

That really caught Sally off guard. "What?" She searched his eyes for explanation. "Why would you think that?"

"Because you were acting so weird, and unusually forward and horny. I figured cheating was a more likely explanation than alien abduction." Shane laughed but it sounded forced and unconvincing. "Actually it seemed a more likely explanation than your explanation, to be honest. I mean you making out with someone in the library last night would make more sense than you getting so worked up over seeing someone else, you know?" His smile seemed just as forced as the laugh. Sally chuckled quietly, even though his doubt felt like a punch in the gut.

It hurt to think that he had doubted her, but she had to admit that she would probably feel the same if the tables were turned. Since Kate had the same initial suspicion, Sally figured it was warranted. She thought about sharing Kate's reaction but decided against it. "I can understand that, I really can. But I hope you know, deep down, that I would never do that, or anything to hurt you, babe. I'm sorry that I freaked you out."

"I'm not," Shane said with the boyish grin that had melted her heart so many years before, and this time it was sincere. "I'm not sorry at all. I do know I can trust you, so don't worry. And, honestly, I think this might be the best thing that has ever happened to us."

Sally raised her brows, widening her eyes in surprise. "Wow, that's pretty strong."

"It's all about the intensity." Shane grinned as he kissed her on the forehead.

"Well, that sex was certainly intense, right?" Sally squeezed his soft cock. "I just couldn't get enough of you. In fact, I think I could go again." Sally pretended to attempt to clamber on top of Shane.

He held her off. "Whoa, I think I'm down at least until after dinner, babe. A guy needs nourishment and a cock has to recuperate."

Sally giggled as she slapped his chest playfully. "I was just kidding anyway, but good to know that I can hit you up after we eat if I feel like it."

Shane traced a small circle on the top of her shoulder, at the end of her collarbone, through her silky robe. "Did you like watching us in the mirror?"

"Yeah, it was really hot. We should move the dresser to the foot of the bed, or put a big mirror on the wall by the bed." Sally was always planning, ever practical.

Shane kissed her on the side of her forehead. "Good idea."

"I gathered that you liked it, too." Sally settled into the nook of his arm.

"Was it obvious?" Shane joked.

"Yeah, a little." Sally chuckled. "How do you think you'd feel about watching other people?" Sally held her breath, happy she didn't have to look at him while awaiting his response.

"You mean like porn? You know I like porn. But as I recall, you do not. That was before, though. Maybe New Sally likes porn?" Shane tickled her ribs softly through her robe.

Sally wrinkled her nose, even though Shane couldn't see her face, and shook her head. "No, I don't like porn. It's just not nice, the way they treat the women."

"Maybe you should try it again. Our sex today was a lot more like porn sex than it ever was before."

"Maybe," Sally agreed in a distant and dreamy voice. "You might be right. I'd be willing to try."

Shane sighed contentedly, then squeezed her tighter to his chest. "That a girl, babe. We should be open to new experiences."

"I agree." Sally took a deep breath. "Babe? Would you be open to watching *real* people have sex?" Sally surprised herself with the bluntness of the direct question, but Shane hadn't taken the hint when she'd tried to be subtle earlier. She felt Shane's posture stiffen under her weight at the suggestion. She imagined his brow must be wrinkling as he processed the thought.

"Uh, which people? What do you mean?" He seemed to weigh his words, questioning every single one.

"Don't worry, I don't mean peeping in the neighbors' windows." Sally laughed nervously then drew in a deep breath before continuing. *Just say it.* "I mean watching people who like to be watched."

"Good, because I definitely would not want to see Mr. and Mrs. Jacobs having sex," Shane joked about the elderly couple next door. "But, seriously? You're suggesting that we watch real people having sex? You are dirtier than I ever imagined."

"Vanilla, but dirty." Sally kissed his shoulder.

"Vanilla? Where'd that come from?"

"Kate. She said I was so vanilla I didn't even know I was vanilla. Which I guess was true."

"There's nothing wrong with vanilla, babe."

"But dirty vanilla might be more fun."

"I won't argue with that." Shane squeezed her around the waist and kissed the top of her head. "But who are these people you speak of? People who want to be watched?"

"I don't know, but I'm sure they're out there." No sooner had she finished the sentence that the doorbell rang. Sally jumped up and ran out to pay for the food, leaving Shane to ponder what she had implied. His cock twitched under his robe.

~

Follow Sally and Shanes's erotic escapades in *Two to Tango*.

And if you're dying to see what the wild child sister is up to… Get her story now in *Taming Kate*. Keep reading to check out the first few chapters.

If you like my naughty words, you can get exclusive content and be the first to know about my releases and sales in my newsletter over at MacyButler.com.

If you dare, come join the Racy Readers group over on Facebook. You're forewarned though… it can get more than a little crazy in there, in the crazy-fun sense.

TAMING KATE

EXCERPT

hapter 1

Kate

I scanned the hotel bar for any of my colleagues on my way in. Thank God, it was clean. They'd all been too afraid of Adelaide to show their faces until morning. I slid onto a barstool and grinned at the tattooed bartender.

She flashed me a smile. "What's your pleasure, beautiful?"

The idea of a whiskey had been ruined by the guy in the aisle seat on the plane. "Hendricks and tonic. And do you have cucumber, by chance?"

"Of course I do. Want some rosemary to go with it?" Her eyes lit up with her smile.

"Ah, you know the subtleties of a good G&T. Yes, please." I sat back and watched her mix my drink, complete with Fever-Tree tonic, the very same drink Jordan used to mix for me.

"Thanks, you make me feel like I'm home." I eagerly snatched the drink from her hand before she could set it in front of me.

"Where'd you learn to drink Hendricks with cucumber and rosemary?"

"Oh, my boyfriend was a bartender."

She smiled and leaned onto folded arms on the bar in front of me. "What does he do now?"

I pushed the cocktail straw aside and sipped from the glass, pressing my lips together as I nodded in appreciation at the quality of the drink. "He's still a bartender."

"You said, 'was.' I thought you meant..."

"No, he *was* my boyfriend. I guess I should have said 'ex-boyfriend.' We just broke up last week."

"Oh, I'm sorry. I didn't mean to pry." She glanced down at the bar she was wiping.

"No, it's no big deal. I dumped him." I shrugged. The hardest part about the breakup had been trying to explain it to Jordan. He hadn't done anything wrong. In fact, he tried hard to do everything right. Too hard. But after the initial thrill of the hot sex wore off, I slowly lost interest. How do you make yourself fall in love with someone? I hadn't figured that one out yet.

"Oh, good. Well, here's to greener pastures." She poured herself a half-shot of tequila and held it up toward me.

"Indeed." I agreed even though it was hard to imagine a greener pasture than Jordan. He was hot. He was sweet. And he loved me more than anyone I'd even been with. And yet, I needed more. I needed him to need me less. His devotion had become unattractive. How fucked up was that? How fucked up was I? There was something wrong with me. She didn't need to hear any of that, though. "How long have you been in Vegas?"

"All my life." She shrugged before she placed the shot glass in the sink behind the bar.

"Wow, a Vegas local. You're a rare breed."

"You said it. What brings you to my town?"

My gaze inched up her tattooed sleeve and past the strap of her black tank to her face. The work extending from her elbow up to her shoulder was brilliant. Someone skilled had inked her. I shook my head and blinked to focus on her question. "A work convention. I bet it's the first time you've heard that all night."

"Oh yeah, never heard that one before." Her blue eyes peeked from underneath a black fringe of bangs to meet my gaze.

It wasn't easy to make small talk with her staring into my eyes. I don't even like girls, like that. But she was something. I hoped I didn't sound as awkward as I felt. "What's your favorite drink to mix?"

The bartender was pensive. "Hmm. That's a tough one. I like a challenge. Like a Harvey Wallbanger or something outside the norm. But, really, my favorite is a simple G&T where I can add the subtleties, as you said. A little rosemary. A little cardamom. Fresh vanilla beans. Rose petals."

I smiled as I sipped my drink, feeling giddy and somehow connected like she'd actually *gotten* me and my drink. "Sometimes the little things make all the difference." I felt my chin dip while holding her gaze. My face flushed with embarrassment when I realized what I was doing—flirting. I couldn't help myself. Not because I was attracted to her, per se, but because it's who I am. Especially with bartenders, apparently. I'd only been single for six days and had no desire to hook up with anyone, especially not a woman. But I couldn't help myself from engaging in the game. The rush of capturing someone's attention and making them want me—that was addictive. It was power.

Something brushed my right elbow, pulling my attention from the raven-haired bartender to interrupt my contemplation on my flirtatious nature. The subtle scent of an expensive cologne drifted over from the suited figure who'd saddled up to the barstool beside me, despite several others being open.

"Sometimes it's the bigger things that make the real difference."

I gave him the side-eye. *Really*? Was this Mister Tall Dark and Handsome just going to butt in on our conversation with a big dick reference? "Size is overrated." I turned back to the bartender and rolled my eyes.

"Said no woman ever." His sarcasm was comical.

I turned to face him, and dammit if his dark eyes didn't nearly paralyze my tongue for a second. I smirked. "I just did."

"But you didn't mean it." Confidence oozed from his pores as he broke my gaze to order a drink. "Macallan, neat." He flashed a smile. "That's a nice tat there, Angela." He read her name from the name tag pinned on her shirt that I hadn't noticed until then. *Totally on top of his game.* A player, for sure. Vegas was full of them. He'd fit right in.

"What are you having?" He eyed the sprig of rosemary in my glass.

"A gin and tonic." My answer was short in an attempt to shut him up.

"Oh, a G&T girl, are you? Gin makes women crazy." His remark made me want to smack him, but the way his lips curled into a smile made my body betray me with sparks between my thighs.

"Maybe gin makes crazy women more sane." I forced a grin that I hoped seethed of sarcasm.

"I like crazy. But most men can't handle it." He raised the drink that Angela set in front of him. "Here's to crazy, however it comes."

I studied his smile. He was hard to hate. I lifted my glass to meet his as I stammered for a retort that might throw him off his game. "You can't handle my kind of crazy."

He came back smug as ever. "I've never met crazy I couldn't handle."

I turned with a smirk,"You've never met me," before I turned to face Angela.

"Not yet. What's your name?" Amusement danced in his dark eyes.

I tried to keep a resting bitch face despite the smile that threatened to spread across my lips as I answered dryly. "Kate. Yours?"

"Zayne."

I let my gaze linger on his extended hand before I turned

back to Angela, who seemed amused behind the bar. "Some guys pretend to think they know women."

Her smiling eyes told me she thoroughly enjoyed seeing me leave him hanging like that. "Most guys pretend to think they know everything. Sometimes we play along."

Chapter 2

Zayne

After an eleven-hour flight, the last thing I was looking for was an argument, but the cute brunette at the bar seemed ripe for one. And the bartender seemed to be on her side. They didn't know who they were dealing with, though. I was the king of barroom banter after nearly two decades of training in London. "Some of us don't have to pretend."

I saw the annoyance as she rolled her eyes back toward the bartender, pretending not to see me. Kate was bothered. And because I'm a sadistic bastard, that pleased me immensely. I didn't even try to hide my smug smile as I sipped my drink.

"Where are you coming from?" The bartender turned on her charm, always vying for the tip. There were some things about America that never ceased to amaze me. Wait staff and bartenders in the UK were paid a living wage, so customers weren't expected to cover their salaries. Of course that meant that the service was often surly since they weren't motivated to kiss ass, but I preferred it. It was more honest. It was just one of the many cultural differences that I was going to have to get used to again.

"London. I just flew in, actually."

"Jolly good," Angela replied in a poor imitation accent while Kate continued to ignore me.

"Ahh, you've been to London, then?"

"Not yet, but someday..."

"Eh, it's just New York with an accent. If you're going to travel, I'd put many cities before it on the list if I were you. Paris, Rome, hell, even fucking Madrid."

"I want to see them all. Just saving my pennies." Still working for the tip. I had to smile. But still nothing from Kate who sipped her drink down to the ice. My eyes trailed up her delicate yet muscular arm to a lovely face. Her classic beauty and giant green eyes were reminiscent of a young Elizabeth Taylor. There was a softness about her that she hid quite well underneath a hardened shell—a shell I wanted to crack because I like a challenge.

"How about you, Kate? Have you traveled much?"

"A bit. I did a few weeks in Europe after college. I didn't see London, though. But I *loved* Madrid." Her sly smile confirmed that she wanted to be contrary, which I appreciated. *A bit of a brat, are you?*

"To each her own." I tipped my glass toward hers but she eyed her empty drink. Was she inviting me to buy her a drink? She was hard to read. "Another G&T?"

She licked her full lips and took a second to think about it. I couldn't help but imagine those lips in other places. I shifted to ease the tension of my growing cock on my zipper as she finally shrugged. "Sure, why not?"

Good answer.

Kate avoid looking my way while the bartender popped the

top off the bottle of premium tonic water as she mixed Kate's drink. I liked that she avoided eye contact. It meant I had some sort of effect on her. I leaned onto my elbow with a grin. "So, tell me, what did you like about Madrid?"

Kate shrugged, her eyes flitting toward me only briefly. "It's beautiful. The palace. The food. The clubs. The men. What's not to love?" There was a playful spark in her fiery gaze when turned. She liked being contrary.

"What did you like about Spanish men?" The disdain in my voice might have been a little overdone.

Kate laughed under her breath and rolled her eyes. "They're handsome, and gentlemen,"—her eyes narrowed as they leveled on mine—"and not at all cocky." That little jab added to my suspicion that she was a class-A brat. At least now I knew what she thought she didn't like about me. I could make her like it. I wasn't planning on a game of cat and mouse after the day I'd had, but she'd drawn me into it.

"You shouldn't confuse confident for cocky." I swirled the whiskey in my glass.

"You shouldn't make assumptions about women you don't know." She picked up the drink Angela set in front of her. "I know cocky when I see it."

She was tough. "Let me get this straight. You fancy yourself crazy, like that's a good thing. And I'm cocky, presumably a bad thing."

"You're catching on." A hint of a smile crept across her sweet little lips before she sipped her drink. "I *fancy myself* crazy in the wild-and-crazy sense, not in the certifiable-or-batshit sense."

Her mocking my British-sounding word choice was oddly

arousing. "That's good. Wild and crazy sounds like fun. Batshit crazy does not."

Her confidence trumped mine in her retort. "Not that you'll ever know, but I'm wicked fun."

"That I don't doubt." And oh yes, I would know. Sooner than later. Challenge accepted.

Chapter 3

Kate

Was this guy for real? He took cocky to a whole new level. Most guys back down when I call them on their shit, but Zayne seemed to enjoy it.

With the body of an athlete and the face of a God he had every reason to be cocky. His fitted designer dress shirt and tailored slacks hugged the contours of his very tall and muscular frame. Chiseled cheekbones and a square jawline framed dark brown eyes with long thick lashes every woman would envy. His presence commanded attention. And his energy demanded it. Which is exactly why I was determined to ignore him, and also why I couldn't. It didn't help that the bar had filled up, so Angela was busy, which meant I couldn't use her to escape. I could feel his eyes still on me as I fiddled with the rosemary garnish in my drink.

"What are you doing in Vegas?"

I sighed. "A work conference."

"Oh yeah? What do you do?"

I held up my hand to put a stop to his line of questioning. "Please. I'm stuck here with my whole department for three days. I don't even want to *think* about work right now, let alone talk about it."

He shrugged. "Fair enough. What do you want to talk about then?"

I was tempted to say "Nothing" but I was enjoying the banter. "Why don't you tell me about you? I bet that's your favorite subject."

ACKNOWLEDGMENTS

Thanks, especially, to my two sons who have encouraged me to follow my writing dreams even if it means less family time sometimes.

Also many thanks to my BFF's Amanda and Keri who were my first beta readers and the first IRL friends to know my dirty secret (writing steamy romance).

A big shout out and THANK YOU to a multitude of budding and already-established authors who have shared their knowledge with me along the way. I hope I can pay it forward one day.

ABOUT THE AUTHOR

Macy is a foul-mouthed tennis addict whose sweet side comes out with her two teenage sons. She loves to write about sassy women who like their men Alpha in the bedroom and Beta at the breakfast table. Strong, smart heroines inspire her as much as hard-bodied heroes with hearts of gold.

Macy loves to create stories to enhance a couple's sensual and emotional connection. Through characters ballsy enough to push their own boundaries to cross the line from fantasy to reality, Macy hopes to inspire readers to think outside the confines of social norms.

When she's not on the tennis court or locked in her writing cave, you'll find Macy on the beach with a sunset cocktail or out on the boat near their home in the Florida Keys.

Connect with Macy, and get exclusive content and special offers at www.macybutler.com

- Website: www.macybutler.com
- Twitter: https://twitter.com/MacysRacyReads
- Instagram: https://www.instagram.com/macysracyreads/
- Facebook: www.facebook.com/macybutlerauthor/
- Macy's Racy Readers Group: www.facebook.com/groups/411914929595690/
- Goodreads: http://bit.ly/MacyButler
- Bookbub: www.bookbub.com/authors/macy-butler
- TikTok: https://www.tiktok.com/@macybutlerauthor

Made in the USA
Coppell, TX
02 December 2021

66895534R00063